MW01623048

GENESIS: THE REBIRTH

M. E. Richey

Baltimore, Maryland

GENESIS: The Rebirth

Library of Congress
Cataloging in Publication Data
ISBN 1-56167-562-8

Library of Congress Card Catalog Number:
99-067016

Published by

8019 Belair Road, Suite 10
Baltimore, Maryland 21236

Manufactured in the United States of America

Main Characters

Kate Malloy	Secretary of the Assistant to the President on the National Security Council
Reed Adams	Investigative Reporter and Television News Talk Show Host
General Brad Powers	Commander in charge of Base Operations at the Pentagon
Helene Powers	Wife of General Brad Powers, and Professor at Georgetown University
Diane Powers	Daughter of Brad and Helene, friend of Kate Malloy
Willard Hastings	President of the United States
Jessica Hastings	First Lady
Jason Betts	Assistant to the President on the National Security Council

Preface

This book was written for the express purpose of entertainment. But, it is also my desire to awaken the minds of people to the workings of the government, and nudge their interest toward monitoring the work of their elected leaders. We must remember that the United States is a free republic, and that our president and elected leaders are supposed to be working for the good of the people, not for their own power and greed. We must be ever watchful and make sure that our freedoms stay intact.

Never think that this country is above having a leader who has grandiose ideas of staying in power. Never think for one minute that it can't happen here in the United States of America.

Chapter 1

Jolted awake from a frightening nightmare, Kate Malloy sat up in bed and tried to get her bearings. Having broken out in a cold sweat, she sat shivering as visions of her terror-filled dream came racing back. She saw herself running at top speed, trying to distance herself from the evil threat that pursued her. Her briefcase was swinging wildly as she sped along. Gasping for air, she turned and glanced over her shoulder. Her pursuer was gaining fast and she could see the shiny black object in his hand. Making a quick turn, she heard the crack of a gun being fired as she tore down a residential side street. She sensed the man was after her because of the briefcase. She was intent on getting to a specific destination, but where that was, she had no idea. Her legs were giving out and she had no breath left to go on. Just as she heard another crack, she woke with a start.

Kate sat there on the bed with both arms wrapped tightly around her knees. This nightmare was identical to one she had about a month ago. She took a deep breath and gazed out the window of her ninth floor apartment. Below she could hear the hum of traffic and knew it was time to get up and get ready for work.

Putting thoughts of her bad dream out of her head, she swung her five-foot-seven, athletic body out of bed and headed for the shower. The soothing water flowing over her relaxed her tense muscles.

Kate had learned long ago to trust her dreams and feelings. She knew that her repeated nightmare was trying to warn her of impending danger, but danger from what or whom she didn't know. As she finished her shower and proceeded with dressing, she thought of the other times that she had sensed unpleasant happenings. Some were of a personal nature, such as the time she envisioned her parents' fatal automobile accident. At other times, she perceived, through dreams or visions, disasters such as earthquakes or floods.

After doing research on the subject, she acknowledged the fact that she was one of a gifted few that were known as "Sensitives." These were people who could actually feel the forces of outside influences using a form of extra sensory perception.

Sitting at her dressing table brushing her golden brown hair into a flowing style, she put her misgivings aside and turned her thoughts to the present. Taking a last critical check of herself in the mirror, her dark green eyes sparkling with flecks of gold, she gave a quick nod and headed for the kitchen for her usual cup of coffee, some juice and a Danish. She would take her newspaper with her to work and check out the headlines and major stories at her desk.

After graduating college, Kate worked for five years doing political research in the Washington office of her state senator, David Allen. Her major had been political science because of her avid interest in politics and government. She had applied herself well and ended up in the top two percent of her class.

A year ago, she applied for and was accepted to fill the position of secretary to the president's assistant on the National Security Council. She had supported the president's party and felt that he was just what this country needed, and agreed with most of his policies. During his first term and most of the way through his second, everything good seemed to prevail. Unemployment was at an all time low and the economy was booming. Americans were happy with their president and credited him alone for their good life.

So, when election time rolled around once again, the good citizens, lulled into a complacent sense of security, put him snugly back in office, and with the opposition party in Congress bowing to the president's every wish, it was as though the nation was under a one-party system. Now, into the last months of his second term, serious problems were arising. It looked as though the country was taking the proverbial nose-dive. More and more jobs were being lost due to big companies moving lock, stock, and barrel to foreign shores. Taxes were shooting up, the stock market was in a daily decline, and there was unprecedented crime in the country.

Citizens who were previously lethargic to government's activity, due to their good life and plenty of money in their pockets, were becoming fearful, angry, and disillusioned. And Kate was one of them. Now, after working in the White House for a year, she was having great misgivings about Willard Hastings. She had been noticing subtle, slow changes being put into effect; changes that were contradictions to the president's campaign promises.

She began a few months ago making notes on questionable executive orders that were making their way through Congress with hardly a second look and were now law. She also took note of documents that passed through her office that had underlying subversive procedures included in some obscure passage.

By now she had amassed quite a file full of factual materials from research and documents. Things were starting to happen at a greater rate of speed, not only on the home front, but the world over.

Eager to start the day, Kate arrived at the White House gate and presented her pass to the guard.

"Mornin', Kate, ready for a busy day?"

"Always ready to do battle," she answered with a grin. "Hope your day is uneventful, Jim," and gave him a little salute as she headed for her office.

She continued to think about her compilation of facts and wondered what exactly she was going to do with the information. She had no idea, but would jump that hurdle when she came to it. For now , she would just continue as she had been. She fortified her resolve to continue making them believe she was still a game player. Knowing that she had earned trust and respect from her boss, she had no worries about being suspect. Showing no discontent in anyone's presence, and performing her job with vigor and enthusiasm, Kate was acknowledged as a loyal party member.

It had been a jolt to her senses when she became aware of the underhanded tactics, lies, and subversive actions of her chosen official.

She recalled her first encounter with an executive order that Hastings had issued, suspending a previous executive order which gave the individual states the right to define the moral, political, and legal character of their lives. In suspending that order, he took away those states' rights and delegated them to himself.

Kate remembered how upset she felt at the time. Thinking that Congress would indeed reject the suspension order, she unhappily found out that it went through without even a whimper.

Her feelings were that the president was usurping the Constitutional rights of the states to govern themselves. She didn't like the federal government having more continued control, for it took the power away from the people and their elected state leaders. It removed the power of the people to vote on issues pertinent to their own areas.

It was from that point on that she decided to keep a close watch on other presidential edicts, and there were many, flowing through at a tremendous rate of speed.

Other orders, such as the Implementation of Human Rights Treaties, tried to bypass the ratification by the Senate and give this power to the United Nations.

And yet another asserts plenary and dictatorial authority over citizens, food, transportation, energy, health, contracts, materials and resources, to be exercised by the National Security Council and FEMA.

Never hearing about them through the media or newspapers, there was no way that she or the rest of the country would or could have knowledge of their existence. Many seemed to have harmless context, but mixed in betwixt and between, she found systematic perpetuation of presidential power.

She had never met the president or first lady up close and personal. Up till now, it had always been at a distance, or in a room full of people. She had occasion to attend a few gatherings at which they both made brief appearances, and, of course, she was on hand at different briefings, if her boss needed her to attend.

"One of these days I'm bound to meet him," she mused.

With that thought she stepped through the doorway of her office, put her purse away and started preparing her work for the day ahead. Silently she hoped it would prove to be an informative, productive one.

There was to be a presidential briefing that evening, and her boss had to participate, so the day would be pretty much taken up with gathering facts that would hopefully cover the array of questions asked by the press. For the next few hours, she busied herself typing up data sheets and making sure that the list her boss had given her was taken care of step by step.

About eleven o'clock, she phoned her close friend and neighbor, Diane, and they agreed to meet at a specified restaurant for lunch. Diane worked at the Library of Congress and was in charge of "Thomas," their new Internet on-line service.

The girls met at the front of the restaurant and proceeded inside to a booth.

"You look great today, Diane. Something tells me there's a big evening ahead. It wouldn't have anything to do with a certain special man in your life, now would it?"

"You're right on both counts," Diane laughed. "There is a big evening planned, and it is with Joe. He's picking me up at work and we're going out for dinner. He landed a very prominent corporation to his clientele, and we're celebrating."

The waitress came to take their orders, then Kate continued, asking how Joe's law practice was doing. Joe Burnett had been a junior partner in a large law firm, but had just recently struck out on his own. He and Diane had been dating regularly for a couple of years now. Diane filled Kate in on how Joe had bagged the job as legal counsel for the giant industry. Their food delivered, the two friends turned their attention to their lunch.

"By the way, Kate, Joe and I have been invited to have dinner at my parents' house on Sunday, and they have also invited you, if you're free."

"I'd love to go. You know how much I enjoy your parents. They always have such interesting and sometimes intriguing stories to relate."

"Okay then, I'll let my mother know to expect us. You can ride with Joe and me. Oh yes, there will also be another guest, a friend of theirs who is a news correspondent for one of the large newspapers in the country and also has a weekly news talk show on ABS."

When Diane said his name, Kate recognized it immediately. Reed Adams was not only very handsome, but he had a knack for fact-finding, and was known for his honesty and integrity. He never held back, whether it was for or against the administration.

"It sounds as if it will be a very enjoyable time, and I'm looking forward to it," Kate said as she gulped down the last of her coffee.

The two paid their check then headed out the door.

"I'll give you a buzz tomorrow and let you know what time we'll leave on Sunday. And Kate, dress casual."

"All right, Diane, and tell your mom thanks for inviting me."

On the way back to the office, Kate thought of the fondness she had for Diane's parents, Brad Powers and his wife Helene. Both seemed to be of the same mind about the president's actions as she, and were sources for some of the data in her file. The general held a prominent position at the Pentagon, directly in charge of base operations. He previously headed the Strategic Missile Defense, until recently, when he was reassigned.

Helene was a tenured professor at Georgetown University. Her expertise was in computer technology, and she often worked with Federal Agents helping them with cases of computer fraud, coding, and the more recent problems with hackers.

Back at her desk again, with the prospect of an interesting weekend ahead, Kate set about the rest of her day's work. Her boss, Jason Betts, came by her desk about four-thirty.

"Kate, do you have the data ready for me to take to the briefing?"

Betts, a shifty little man with darting eyes, often set her on edge with his uncanny way of materializing out of nowhere. With his whiny, neurotic nature, he was not an easy person to work for.

"Yes, sir, here's everything you requested," handing up the data sheets for him to peruse.

After he scanned through them, he gave her a quick nod, turned and headed out the door. Betts was not one to say thank you, as Kate well knew, for she had yet to hear it or any word of praise in the year she had been working for him.

She had about a half hour before she checked out for the day, so she straightened up her desk. That done, she made her way to Betts' inner office. One of her everyday duties was to set his office in order, check his agenda and set out any necessary materials he would need the following day. This being Friday, however, would just entail organizing his desk for Monday, and as far as she knew, nothing was scheduled.

As Kate shuffled the folders around, a small piece of paper fell to the floor. Picking it up to replace it in the folder, her eyes scanned it briefly. It simply said "Genesis, meeting, nine." As she worked on, her mind centered back on the peculiar little message. She couldn't help but wonder why all the secrecy. She always set up Betts' meetings herself, and this is one she knew nothing about, and what or where was "Genesis"?

"Possibly it's a new hotel or restaurant in the area," she surmised, making a mental note to keep her ears open for any mention of the name.

Finally, everything in order, she glanced around and, satisfied, went back to her desk, gathered up her purse and car keys and left for the day. Checking out with the security guard, she wished him a good night.

"See you on Monday, Jim. Enjoy your time with the family," and with a smile continued on her way to the parking lot.

By the time she arrived home, after a stop at the market, she was ready for a soothing hot bath. She decided to do just that, and would fix herself a quick dinner later. Just before she was about to step into the tub, the phone rang. Answering, she heard Bill's voice on the other end. Bill Towner was a likable guy that she dated on occasion. He worked at the Smithsonian Institute, in the area dedicated to flight.

"Have you made any plans for tomorrow night, Kate?"

"No, Bill, I was just going to get some housework caught up."

"I thought you might like to see that new movie that everyone's raving about. They say it's a real chiller and guaranteed to bring goose bumps."

"Sure, how can I pass up an invitation like that? Bet you're also going to guarantee me a post movie nightmare?"

She heard him laugh, then he said, "I'll be around to pick you up at seven-thirty."

"I'll be ready, and thanks for thinking of me."

With that they said their good-byes, and Kate added some hot water to her cooling bath and climbed in to soak.

Refreshed and wearing her comfortable robe, she headed for the kitchen, flipping on the television as she went past. The president's briefing was due to air shortly, and she tried never to miss one.

As she waited she poured herself a goblet of white zinfandel wine and popped an Italian dinner in the microwave. Ready in a few minutes, she took her food and wine into the den, where she often ate while watching press conferences, briefings and the like. She felt it was part of her job to keep up to the minute on everything coming out of the White House.

This briefing had to do with the volatile situation erupting in the Balkans. With cameras riveted on the door from which President Hastings would emerge, the commentators continued to make small talk.

Within the minute, the president appeared and following him was her boss and General Langwell. The general was in charge of troop deployment and operational tactics. Kate always marveled at how controlled and relaxed the president was in front of the cameras. He had an appealing smile which tended to make everyone feel at ease in his presence.

Kate gave a little half smile when she thought of some of the stories floating around the White House, told by some members of the president's and first lady's staff. Seems that they were witness to some violent arguments between the two over affairs of State. Though the first lady, Jessica, kept busy with programs such as children's education and women's rights, she was also very involved in government policies. And to all reports, she was not one to run afoul of, since her wrath could be even more devastating than that of the president.

This pleasant-looking man, who she was viewing on her television screen, was capable of tirades and fits of anger the likes that have never been seen by his voting public. Even Kate had heard a few of his rantings echoing down the halls near her office. But here he was, the very essence of composure.

Her boss, on the other hand, acted edgy and shifted from one foot to another whenever he stepped up to the microphone to address a question.

The camera panned to the different members of the press as they posed what they imagined were pertinent questions. Kate couldn't help but wonder how most of them earned their credentials, due to the vapid, inane questions they would blurt out.

More than half way through the briefing, however, a deep calm voice arose from the group. Kate, recognizing it, sat up as the camera moved to catch sight of the speaker.

She admired the aggressiveness and forthright way of speaking that Reed Adams had, although she thought of him as a bit of a rogue, and heaven knew, he was not well thought of by many at the White House. She was always hearing her boss complain about Adams' constant digging and probing into things that were none of his business.

He was addressing a question to the president, and she leaned forward in her chair.

"Mr. President, why have you taken this aggressive action of deploying thousands of our troops into a confrontation of ethnic battles within the country of Macedonia? And, as a follow up, how do you justify it as being in the best interests of the United States?"

The president turned to Reed with a look that said "not this pesky gnat again." He answered in a condescending tone, trying to state his valid reasons for having our forces there. Something about the two warring factions being a threat to neighboring countries and should other countries start siding with one cause or the other, it would most assuredly cause widespread chaos and would have a dire effect on the world trade.

Kate could see by the expression on his face that Reed wasn't buying such gibberish, and to tell the truth she was hard pressed to see the sense of it all.

This decision to deploy our troops into a war zone was not passed through Congress for approval, but was a direct order from the president. He had issued an executive order, that had been ignored by Congress, like so many of them were, giving the president the power to carry out deployment of troops in times of crisis, when there would be no time for Congress to vote, with the intent of surprise action.

Some in Congress were crying foul, but they had no one to blame but themselves for not paying attention to executive orders that came to them for approval or rejection. Now some were objecting harshly that our troops had no business over there.

Not only were our men and women in Macedonia fighting and dying on foreign soil, but the president had sent well over a million of our armed forces into many far off countries, in conjunction with the United Nations, to keep peace. We literally had nothing but a shadow of militia on our home shores.

Soon after the briefing ended, Kate took her dishes to the kitchen, stuck them in the dishwasher, grabbed a big sweater to throw over her robe, and made her way out on the balcony off the living room. She felt a cold breeze as she stood at the half wall that surrounded it. Glancing off to her right, she could see the dark waters of the Potomac flow along quietly in the hush of the night. Straight ahead was a soft glow emanating from the Lincoln Memorial.

She thought of how peaceful this night was, and she thought about Reed Adams.

Chapter 2

Saturday dawned, and Kate rose and made her way to the kitchen. Mentally, she went over her day's schedule as she ate her breakfast and glanced through the morning paper.

She came upon Reed's column and read his scathing report, condemning the president for his rash decision to deploy troops into a war arena. Kate liked the way he reasoned and thought that she certainly was looking forward to meeting this man.

She kept herself busy all day with grocery shopping, washing clothes, and cleaning her apartment.

About mid-afternoon, Diane stopped by to chat and to give her a time for the Sunday dinner. Getting up to leave, she reminded Kate that she and Joe would stop by for her.

About six o'clock, she thought she had better start dressing for her movie date with Bill. She was ready and waiting when the doorbell chimed, and when she opened the door, Bill scurried in.

"Hi, Kate, hope you're prepared for a thriller of a movie."

Kate laughed. "You know how I love a good scary movie, Bill, as long as it has a good plot to go along with the chills and thrills. Would you care for a glass of wine before we leave?"

"Think I'll wait till we get back. We're running a little late, and I don't want to miss the start of it."

"I'll grab my coat then, and we'll get going," she said over her shoulder as she started for the closet.

"You look great tonight, as usual, Kate," Bill said as they made their way out to where he had parked his car.

"Thanks and how are things going at the Institute?" she asked.

"The crowds are thin, as happens in the winter months. We've received a couple more acquisitions for our area and I've been busy getting them set up. I'm trying to get everything in order by year's end. It doesn't seem possible that in less than a month the year two thousand will be upon us."

"And with that, the prospect of Y2K problems," Kate replied. "However, I know that the White House is more concerned with terrorists' attacks at that vulnerable time, rather than any computer glitches that may occur," she added.

"It'll be an interesting time in history, for certain," Bill exclaimed as they pulled into the theater parking area.

Within a few minutes they had their tickets and found seats to their liking. The movie proved to be everything Bill had predicted and when it ended, Kate stated so.

"That's nightmare material if I ever saw it," she laughed.

On the ride home they talked about the movie and Bill asked Kate what was new at the White House.

"Just the usual paperwork and rushing to meet appointments. Coming up next week I have to accompany Mr. Betts to a hearing before the Congressional Committee on Foreign Affairs. They're making inquires into this latest war action, and the boss wants me there to have the backup materials at hand. For the next few days I'll be preparing the data sheets. Poor Mr. Betts is not looking forward to the grilling that is bound to come from some of the opposition on the Committee," she added with a grin. "Also, I have some reference work to do for the press secretary."

Kate and Bill's relationship was strictly a companionable one, and Kate never talked about anything other than generalities. She never cared to divulge any of her inner thoughts and fears to him.

They soon arrived back at her apartment, and Kate invited him in for his previously forsaken glass of wine. Taking their drinks into the den, they spent the next half hour enjoying each other's company.

Bill got up, stretched, and announced that he'd best be getting along home. She walked him to the door where he gave her a friendly kiss and said his good night. Kate locked up after he left, picked up a book she had started to read, and headed for bed. Reading always cleared her mind, and soon she drifted off into a peaceful sleep, devoid of nightmares.

Sunday proved to be a cold, brisk day. "It looks as though winter is upon us," she mused, as she donned her sweats for her usual Sunday jog. She grabbed her transistor radio, put her earplugs in place, and headed out into the brisk morning air.

As she jogged along she listened to *Meet The Press*. Their guests today were two senators speaking to the issue of the war in Macedonia. One of the senators was David Allen, her previous boss, and senator from her home state.

"Seems that David is against the president's actions," she thought, as she ambled along.

Though he was of the president's party, he was a moderate, and she noted that the senator was in every way, distancing himself from the administration. She was aware of others also who were jumping ship, due to the drastic changes in the president's policies.

On she jogged for a couple more miles, then circled back toward her apartment. She changed over to her favorite music station for the last part of her run. Upon returning home, she freshened up a bit, then sat down to read the Sunday paper.

The headlines were full of war news and of the controversial actions of the administration. They were reporting growing numbers of loss of life to American troops. The article said nothing however, about the worldwide disapproval of the president's invading a sovereign country on the pretext of stopping ethnic slaughter. There was, after all, ethnic slaughter going on in many countries, among those, China and Africa. Seems this president would pick and choose where he wanted to put his armies.

Other stories were about the ever-growing problems of "illegals" making their way across our southern borders, causing those states affected to have an overflow of welfare recipients.

Kate continued on to the most recent breaking story about China pilfering nuclear secret documents from the United States. The president's media had kept mum on the events going on at the time China was stealing our nuclear secrets.

The general public had not been aware of yet another of Hastings executive orders, transferring the authority over exports from the State Department to the Department of Commerce.

It was a move by the president to get the power under his control through the head of the Department of Commerce. The head of the State Department quit his job in protest over this blatant transfer of power.

Once accomplished, the Department of Commerce allowed their favored companies to export computers to China, thereby allowing them to run the software and tests they pulled off a Chinese spy's computer here at our nuclear laboratory in New Mexico.

This was the same spy who was reported to the White House at the time, although the White House took nary a step to check him out. The president didn't want an investigation.

The end result was that the United States had no defense mechanism in place to forewarn of a nuclear attack from China.

On top of that, the president had cut back severely on our nuclear arsenal, while the Chinese were rapidly building nuclear missiles. Now it was suspected that they surpassed the United States in nuclear power.

Until recently, when the cover-up was investigated and reported, the good citizens of the country had been very much kept in the dark. Even as this treasonous act unfolded in bits and pieces, the people were not hearing the information from the mainstream Hastings press.

In recent years, the president had made several trips to China in a so-called effort to bind the two countries. Now, accusations had arisen that those visits were for other purposes.

Kate sat there engrossed in her own thoughts, thinking of the changes that had occurred in just one short year.

She moved on to the comics and then to the Arts and Entertainment section. She spotted an article telling about the gala that the White House was planning in honor of Ivan Belkhanov, the Russian president.

He and his wife Anna would be visiting Washington on December twenty-third. It named the entertainers who would be there and other state dignitaries who were to attend.

Kate had her invitation, and was very much looking forward to it. It would be her first big affair, and she was hoping for a chance to finally meet the president and first lady. Also, she thought, "There may be bits of inside information I might happen to overhear."

Kate had many misgivings about the task she had undertaken, but felt it worthwhile. Since she was in a position to ferret out information, there was no better time to dig out the proof she was seeking. She felt instinctively that something was going on with this president, that would not bode well for the country. There was something very wrong, and she had to find out what that was.

Before she realized it, the day had flown by, and wanting to give herself extra time to get ready and dressed for her dinner with the Powers, she began the task of deciding what she would wear.

Since the weather had turned cold, her choice was a pair of cream slacks and a pale olive green sweater set. That done, she headed for the shower, and soon was towel-drying her hair at her dressing table.

Before long, she was dressed and had her hair pulled back in a flattering, sophisticated style. She clasped a gold pendant around her neck, and put small gold earrings in place. Pleased with her efforts, she glanced at the time and realized that Diane and Joe would be coming around soon.

No more than thinking that, the doorbell chimed. Opening the door, she was met with two smiling faces. They stepped in while Kate made a last check around, then picking up her coat and purse, they were on their way.

She liked Joe, and knew that his and Diane's relationship had moved to the serious stage. She was happy for her friend, and knew that wedding bells were not far off.

The three of them chattered happily away and shortly pulled up in front of the Powers' residence. In front of them was a sleek little sports car, and Kate thought it most likely belonged to Reed Adams.

The trio made their way in the front door and were met by Helene. After giving her daughter a hug, she turned to greet Joe and Kate. She ushered them into the living room where the general and Reed were in quiet conversation.

Both men stood, and since Kate was the only one who hadn't met Reed, the general introduced them.

"Miss Malloy, a pleasure to meet you," Reed uttered.

"Please, call me Kate," she returned and reached out to shake his hand.

"Kate," he responded.

She could feel the energy in his handshake, but she also noted a guarded look as his eyes held hers. She finally broke free, turned and spoke to the general. In the back of her mind she was pondering her cool reception from Reed, most likely, she told herself, it was because of her position at the White House. It was certainly no secret that Reed was in opposition to the president and his recent actions. No doubt he believed her to be in sympathy to this administration.

The general's voice brought Kate back to the present.

"How've you been, Kate? It's been a while since we've had the pleasure of your company."

"I'm fine, General, it has been a while, but I guess we've all been busy these days. I'm happy to be here tonight to catch up on all the news that you two always have to share," she added.

The little group made themselves comfortable, the general having made them each a mixed concoction of their choice, and soon they were all exchanging stories on the latest happenings in their lives.

Reed was quite at home, and it even seemed to Kate that he was thawing out some where she was concerned. She was intrigued with him, and had to admit that she was experiencing quite a physical attraction to him.

"What an enigma he is," she thought.

She imagined that many other women felt the same toward him and wondered if there was any one special lady in his life. Ever so often she would glance his way and find his eyes focused on her, as if in deep study.

Joe and Diane excused themselves and made their way out to the kitchen to keep Helene company and to see if their assistance was needed.

Reed, the general and Kate kept their conversations light and covered the latest happenings around town— what foreign statesmen were visiting, how the Washington Redskins were faring, and new places to dine. Kate noted that Genesis was not among the few new restaurants that had been mentioned.

Helene entered the room and announced that dinner was on the table. The three of them rose and joined the others in the dining room. Helene asked Kate to take the chair next to Reed, Diane and Joe opposite them, and the general and Helene at each end. Helene said a short blessing, then their attention turned toward filling their plates with the appetizing food that was spread out before them.

The prime rib was roasted to perfection and they all proceeded to enjoy the meal. Dinner conversation was pleasant, with Joe and Diane talking of future plans the two had made.

When the meal was finished and all had more than their fill, Helene poured each a small after dinner cognac. They no sooner rose from the table when Diane's pager beeped. She went to the den to return the call and shortly came out saying that there was a problem with "Thomas," and that she had to return to the office.

"You stay here and enjoy yourself, Kate, and Joe will come back for you after he drops me off at the apartment to pick up my car. It may be a late night, and I don't want to keep him hanging around till I can get the problem solved."

"That's okay," Reed broke in, "you two go ahead and I'll see that Kate gets home when she's ready to leave."

"Oh thanks, Reed, that would be appreciated." And with a quick hug for her parents and a snappy "catch you tomorrow, Kate," Diane and Joe took their leave.

"Would you ladies mind if I absconded with the general for some private talk?" Reed asked, addressing Helene and Kate.

"Not at all, Reed," Helene responded. "Kate and I have a lot of catching up to do ourselves."

The two men retreated to the general's office, and Kate and Helene made their way to a couple of comfortable chairs in the living room. Helene related some of her involvement in the latest investigation of computer hacking. It seems that top secret Pentagon documents had found their way to China.

"The CIA is busy trying to track down the hacker and follow the China trail. Isn't it strange, on the face of things, the president is now touting China as our ally, but behind the scenes, there is more and more covert action in Chinese spy activity," Helene said more as a statement rather than a question.

"Yes, it seems that the president has been ignoring nuclear technology that has found its way to China from the nuclear laboratories here in the United States," Kate replied. "The reports say that China is now in possession of the process we use to build our newest strategic missile warheads. I'm fast becoming wary of the president's actions, which have taken a U-turn from previous policies. Of course, I keep those thoughts to myself around the office. I don't think the administration would take lightly to a dissident in their midst," she said with a wry grin.

Moving on to other topics, Kate related to Helene the latest rumors of conflict between the president and first lady.

"Their aides are saying that their confrontations are becoming more violent with each passing day. Seems that the first lady is quite distressed with this latest action. She's looking to the future for her own political possibilities and is aware that the public is very unhappy with the deployment of troops into a war zone."

Putting unpleasant things aside, Kate said "I received an invitation to the gala that's to be held December twenty-third for Mr. Belkhanov and his wife Anna. Will you and the general be attending?"

"Yes, and I'm so happy that you'll be there. We'll be sure to seek you out. Won't this be your first big event, Kate?"

"Uh huh, I've never been to an affair of this magnitude before, and most likely I'll feel like the proverbial fish out of water. A familiar face will be most welcome," she smiled.

They chatted on about what they would wear and who of importance might attend.

Meanwhile, back in the recesses of the general's office, a conversation of a more dire nature was taking place.

"What have you been able to find out, General? Any signs of accelerated movement from the suspected parties?"

"Things are starting to move, Reed; more secret meetings taking place involving the president, General Manning, Betts, Hargraves and Preston. Hastings has got Secret Service standing guard to make sure their meetings are not disrupted." The general continued on. "My guess on this, Reed, is that the president is moving forward, and that whatever he's planning will coincide with Y2K. It's the opportune time to camouflage whatever plot he has in progress."

Reed agreed with him. "Now that he's assembled the National Guard and FEMA as our "homeland" protectors in case of probable disasters such as Y2K and terrorist attacks, his backup is in place."

"Just last week he appointed Mike Preston as commander," the general went on. "And the irony is that Preston, along with the FBI and CIA, will all report directly to Hargraves, the attorney general."

"Yes, it's a nice, neat little package, Reed sneered, since Hargraves takes his orders from the president. My thinking along this line, is that they're planning to place a few bombs in strategic areas of the country; possibly New York City, Los Angeles, San Francisco and maybe even Washington D.C. Bombs that he can blame on Iraqi-backed terrorists."

The general thought that Reed's take on the situation was valid and said as much.

"As far as I can tell, Reed, the vice president isn't a part of this," the general uttered, deep in thought. "The president has had Quinlan globe-trotting on good will junkets, and he hasn't been a part of the secret get-togethers," he added. "He and his wife haven't been around D.C. for weeks, although they'll be returning soon and attending the affair for Belkhanov.

I've got our people in place waiting for orders from me, and others are working on gathering the proof we need. However, they're running into roadblocks because of the tight security."

"Keep them pushing, General, time's growing short and we need to nail this down. We could be barking up the wrong tree, but from where I stand, everything leads to Y2K," Reed finished.

"By the way," he continued, "where do Kate's sympathies lie? You know her. Has she given you any indication which way she's leaning?"

The general was quick to reply. "From the conversations that we've had with Kate, she's turned her alliance away from the White House. She's spoken to both Helene and me about her misgivings, and she's as much concerned as we are that something covert is going on with the president. Her position as Betts' secretary gives her inside access to those close to the president," he added. "She could be of value to us Reed, where Betts is concerned. My guess is that he's the president's number one boy, and if Kate would do a bit of digging, maybe she could come up with something viable."

"General, if you think she can be trusted, I'll try to draw her out on the drive home. It would be asking a lot of her, and might open her up to danger. Let's see how it develops, and I'll let you know what Kate has to say. Now, I think we'd better make our presence known to the ladies; it's growing late, and I'd best get Kate home."

They made their way into the living room and found Helene and Kate still in animated conversation. They looked up when the men walked in and smiled.

"My, but you look like two guys who completely lost track of time," Helene grinned.

The men stood there smiling sheepishly.

"If you're ready, Reed, we'd best be on our way. It's getting quite late, and we all have to work tomorrow," Kate said while rising from her chair.

"Yes, I believe we should get going," Reed agreed.

The two thanked the Powers for an enjoyable time, said their good nights and strolled out into the night.

On the drive home, Reed threw out little questions, trying to get a better insight into Kate's feelings. She realized what he was up to, but answered truthfully, instinctively knowing that she could trust him.

She thought that maybe she had said too much though, and so added, "Reed, I certainly don't want to put my job in jeopardy, so I'm asking you to keep what I say under your hat."

"You have my word, Kate. Whatever you say will stay between the two of us. I'm happy to know that you're smart enough to have figured out that things are going haywire with this president."

They came up on Kate's apartment, and she asked Reed if he would like to come up for a late drink before heading for home.

"Thanks, Kate, but I have an early morning deadline to meet and have to get home and complete my column tonight. I would, however, be pleased if you'd accept an invitation to dinner some night this week. That is, if you're not involved in a serious relationship," he added wistfully.

Kate smiled. "No, there's no one special in my life at present, and I'd be delighted to have dinner with you. How about you coming to my place, and I'll fix dinner here? I'm not sure it'd be a good idea to be seen in public with the 'notorious' Mr. Adams."

Reed agreed to that. "I see your point. If word got back to the White House that their Kate was seen hobnobbing with the enemy, not only would your job be in jeopardy, but it could put you in danger. This president is not above ridding himself of any interference, Kate, and I want you to keep that in mind."

Nodding, she then asked, "Shall we make it Wednesday, about seven? Is there anything special you'd like to eat?"

He told her that he liked most everything, and opted for her to decide. That settled, Kate said good night, and thanked him for the lift home. He walked her up to the front door, said good night, and when she was safely inside, turned and trotted back to his car.

Inside her apartment, Kate kicked off her shoes and gave a little twirl around. She thought, “This evening was more than I expected—oh yes, so much more!”

Chapter 3

Monday morning found Kate scampering around the office collecting the data needed for her boss' appearance before the Congressional Committee.

Unknowingly, the key on her intercom was left open when she passed the deputy assistant's call on to her boss. She heard Betts whining to Paul Robbins. Realizing that the key had been left open, she leaned over to switch it off when the thought hit her that she might pick up some pertinent information, so she left it open.

While keeping an eye on the outer door, should someone enter, she listened quietly to the conversation.

"I don't know why I have to waste my time with these flag-waving politicians! What we need is one party; the president's party. Then we wouldn't have these petty inquisitions to put up with. Little men and women filled with their own importance crying over soldiers losing their lives in Macedonia. Bah! That's what soldiers are supposed to do—fight battles! Mr. Betts, why are our forces in Macedonia? Mr. Betts, isn't this an act of aggression on the part of the United States? Mr. Betts, Mr. Betts, I'm sick of it, Robbins. Soon we won't have to put up with these dissidents. I can't wait till they're put out to pasture, the whole blasted lot of them!"

Kate had heard enough and quickly shut off the intercom. Her mind, reeling from the venom that Betts was spewing, rendered her numb. Shaking herself back to reality, she tried to get a grasp of what she had overheard. Quickly, she jotted down everything while it was still fresh in her mind as if she would forget that repulsive tirade. She put the note away in her briefcase for safe keeping until she got home, then she would spend time studying it more thoroughly.

But for now, she had to get back to the work at hand.

Thinking that she had another day to finish up the committee data, she neatly tucked it away in her desk drawer. Knowing that Greg Hicks, the press secretary, would be coming by later that afternoon for his press conference material, she turned her attention to getting that completed.

Betts had given her a list of informative matters to gather together for Hicks on the troop deployment to Macedonia, and also updates on the peace keeping forces in Bosnia.

A few reporters, that weren't in Hastings back pocket, were starting to question not only the aggressive war action, but why this president had over one and a half million of our armed forces scattered all over the globe. Hicks was having no easy time trying to explain away all of the president's about-faces on his promises.

Her phone rang and Kate picked it up and heard the voice of Gail Thomas, the Deputy Assistant's Secretary.

"How about grabbing something to eat, Kate? It's already past noon, and if we want a good choice of food we should get down there to the cafeteria before it's all picked over. You don't have any other plans, do you?"

"No, Gail, I don't. I can use a break and now would be a good time. I'll meet you at the elevator in two minutes."

Gail was a young, flighty girl who spent most every one of their lunch hours together, either talking about all the "gorgeous hunks" or mooning at them with her big blue eyes. She whiled away the hour on this day, deciding which one of the "hunks" had the cutest buns. Kate liked her though, in spite of the fact that she thought her a bit oxygen impaired.

With lunch over, the two headed back to their respective offices and Kate got back to the pressing task on her desk. She worked along, thinking that she certainly didn't envy Hicks having to face reporters, trying to give valid reasons for the failing economy and the outlandish rise in taxes. With a recession looming and the president's preoccupation with the war and foreign affairs, the people were finally waking up to the fact that we were fast losing the utopian life style of the past.

It was late in the day when Hicks came in to collect his material, then he went in to see if Betts had any late-breaking news that he should know about.

About fifteen minutes later, the two men emerged from the inner office and Betts told Kate he would be leaving for the day.

"I'll need that data for the committee hearing no later than noon tomorrow. I want time to review it," he threw at her as they headed for the outer door.

"It'll be ready, sir," Kate responded.

Before long it was time to leave, so she proceeded through her usual routine of preparing things for the next day's work. Soon she was checked out and on her way home, after a quick stop at the cleaners.

Kate bolted the door behind her, as she always did, and headed to her bedroom to hang up her cleaning. That done, she went to the kitchen and poured a glass of her favorite wine and fixed herself some dinner.

After stacking her dishes in the dishwasher, she went in for a long soak in a hot bath.

An hour later found her opening her briefcase and removing the notes she had made earlier of Betts' telephone conversation. Reading what she had written down almost word for word, she thought that her boss' tirade bordered on treason.

"The man thinks nothing of our service men and women losing their lives, and this talk about not having to put up with Congress—what in the world are they scheming to do? He sounded more like a maniac than a statesman," she mused.

Time was getting late, so, filing the notes away with the other incriminating information she had collected, she went into the bedroom, clicked on her television set and climbed into bed.

She became caught up in watching an old movie that was one of her favorites, *Pandora and the Flying Dutchman.* She thought James Mason and Ava Gardner were at their best as the doomed lovers. The movie all to soon over, Kate, totally relaxed, turned out the light and was soon fast asleep.

The next morning, headlines screamed across every newspaper in the country that Wall Street had hit bottom. The United States was in a recession, as was the rest of the world.

People were in a panic and making a run on the banks, trying to get their money out. The banks had shut their doors and angry citizens were threatening to riot.

The president immediately made a television address to the country, warning the people that there would be dire consequences for any upheaval. He ordered all rioters to disassemble, or arrests would take place. Police were ordered out en masse to keep order in the cities.

Kate was busy manning the phone and contacting countless advisors that Betts needed to talk to. Not only hers, but all offices in and around the White House were being swamped with reporters wanting answers.

The press secretary, Hicks, held a special press conference that afternoon saying that it was not as bad as first expected; things were overstated and the market had leveled off and would soon recover. By evening, things around the country had calmed down, and everyone sat holding their breath, waiting for signs of recovery.

By the time Kate got home there was hardly enough time to eat and soak her tired body in a hot tub of water before turning in for the night.

"Thank heavens Betts told me to come in late tomorrow," Kate murmured, as she fell off in a deep sleep.

Things had quieted down considerably by the time she reached her office, so she took the time to gather all of her material together for the trip over to the halls of Congress.

Early afternoon found Betts, accompanied by Kate, making his way to the Investigative Committee room.

General Langwell had already assumed his position at the head table, and Betts joined him. They both were to give their reports on the war issues, then answer questions that the committee would put to them.

Kate had a seat directly behind Betts, for the purpose of feeding him documents or to reference anything that might be necessary.

As the hearing droned on, she could feel herself getting sleepy and had to fight to keep her wits about her. Betts was not making points with some members of the Committee, and his answers were both clipped and condescending to those who opposed the president's actions.

The hearing finally over, Kate asked her boss if there was any reason for her to return to the office. He waved his hand in a dismissive gesture and told her to go home.

Thankful for the extra time to prepare dinner for Reed, she fairly flew out of the chambers. Driving home, smiling, she figured that Betts was probably on his way to his favorite bar.

At home, she changed into some comfortable slacks and a sweater, and busily put the finishing touches on the meal. Everything under control in the kitchen, she proceeded to set the dining room table in a warm, inviting look, with a small arrangement of fresh-cut flowers as the centerpiece, flanked by three tapered candles.

She was just putting their place settings on when the doorbell announced her visitor. Putting down the dishes, she went to greet her guest.

Reed stood there looking like a school boy picking up his date for the prom. As he stepped in and she closed the door behind him, he handed her a long box, which she opened to find a dozen pale yellow roses.

"They're beautiful, Reed, thank you. Did you know that yellow roses represent hope? They've always been my favorite," she added as she lifted them out of the box and inhaled the sweet scent of them.

"I'd like to take credit for a good guess, but I'm afraid that it was Helene's doing. I phoned her and she happily divulged the information," he stated with a sly grin.

"Well, I'm happy that Helene remembered, and I'm happy that

you asked," she threw back at him as she made her way to the kitchen for a vase. "What would you like to drink? It'll be about ten minutes till we're ready to sit down to eat."

"I'm not a fancy drinker, just some scotch on the rocks, if you have any."

"I'll have to dig around in the back of my cupboard and check. I usually just have wine, but I try to keep a variety on hand for company," she uttered as she stuck her head inside.

Moving bottles around she finally exclaimed, "Hah! I've found some, so you're in luck, my friend."

Reed took his drink and plopped down on a nearby bar stool and watched Kate get their dinner into serving dishes.

"Anything I can do to help?" he offered.

"Can you finish setting our dishes in place? They're on the table. I was about to do that when the doorbell rang."

"Sure thing," and he made his way into the dining room.

Everything ready, Kate put the Cornish hens on a platter, and they sat down to eat. She took pleasant note that Reed had placed their dishes next to one another, instead of at opposite ends of the table, as she had planned to do.

Their conversation during dinner centered on getting to know one another. Questions and answers regarding background, family, and the like were happily supplied by both.

Kate told him that she was from a small town in upstate New York and that her paternal grandparents still lived there. She went on to tell him that she had lived with them since the death of her parents.

Reed related that he was from a large family, five boys and two girls, and that his parents have resided in the same home for almost forty years. He was a middle child, and told some sibling stories that set Kate to laughing. The bulk of his family still lived in Philadelphia, where he was born.

On they talked until they had finished with dessert. With dinner over, Kate rose and blew out the candles and started to clean off the table.

"Let me help you with that," Reed offered. "Living alone, as I do, makes one very handy in the kitchen. And to prove that, you'll have to be my guest on the next occasion."

Kate grinned, said she would like that, and the two made quick work of cleaning up.

Kate fixed Reed another drink and poured herself a goblet of wine. Their drinks in hand, she led the way to the living room. She wished it was warmer so they could go out on the balcony, but the weather had turned blustery and cold, so they each took a seat at opposite ends of the sofa.

Kate kicked off her shoes and brought her legs up and tucked them under her. Reed thought that the time was right to see what she might think about joining their fight.

"Tell me, Kate, just how adamant are you in your misgivings about the president? And what made you change your mind, since you backed Hastings in the past?"

"It was his abrupt change of direction on policies, Reed. I voted for him because I believed he would carry through on important issues that meant a lot to me. Now, things are going on around me that I distrust, and there's a niggling feeling in the pit of my stomach that all is not right where he's concerned, and it won't go away. I know you're not a fan of his, which is obvious from your columns and your talk show. May I ask you why you're so against him?"

"Kate, what I'm going to lay on you may shock you, but this is important for you to hear. First and foremost, this goes no further than this room. That means not even Diane. Her parents do not want her involved in what's going on, and besides, she doesn't show any interest in the workings of government. Are you in agreement?"

"This sounds like something that I ought to steer clear of myself," she said with a little shudder. "But you have my undivided attention and I promise to keep it confidential."

So Reed proceeded to tell her about his working with General Powers and their attempt to find out the plans of the president.

"From all indications, Hastings is working his way toward a takeover of the country. We've suspected it for some time now and have been trying to find out his agenda, but we can't seem to dig up the evidence we need to stop this madness. Whatever his plan, it's a well-kept secret."

Kate's eyes grew larger as she listened without interrupting. At last Reed concluded with what he thought the president might have in mind.

"I believe he may be leaning to the use of terrorist-type bombs, but we have no proof. It's only a theory so far. Kate, the general and I think you could be a great help, having inside access to those close to the president. The general is of the mind that Betts is Hastings' right hand man. What would you think about doing some spying and throwing in with us?"

Kate got up to refill their glasses, not saying anything until she returned and handed Reed his drink.

"Wait here, Reed, I want to show you something."

She went into her bedroom and emerged with a large folder, which she laid down on the coffee table.

Taking the papers out, she handed them to Reed and said, “I’ve already been doing some fact-finding on my own and hadn’t any idea what to do with the information I’ve gathered, but it seems the answer has just been plopped in my lap. For a couple of months now, I’ve been collecting everything that looks suspicious and filing it away. Please, go ahead and take a look at what I have there and see if it’s any help.”

Kate sat quietly while Reed worked his way through the stack of documents and notes.

He sifted through the file, pulling sheets out from the others and stacking them in a separate pile. When he finished, Kate handed him the most recent notes she had made.

“These are from yesterday, when I listened in on a phone call that Betts received from the Deputy Assistant, Robbins. I heard Betts’ end of the conversation over my intercom and was so shocked by what I heard that I made notes.”

She handed Reed the notes and when he finished them, he gave a low whistle.

“Your boss is one ugly thinking man. But this reference to being rid of Congress soon fits in with what we suspect the president has in mind—anarchy.”

He looked up at Kate and asked if she would mind if he took the one stack of separated documents for the general to see.

“You’ve done a terrific job of finding out things that we couldn’t, and it fills in many of the missing pieces to this puzzle. Which leads me to ask whether you are in or out. Can we count on your help?”

“After listening to your suspicions about the president, I’ll do whatever I can to help the cause. And yes, I understand that it might be risky, but Reed, we must do what we can.”

“There’s another area that I find very troubling, having to do with education. From all the factual evidence I’ve been able to get my hands on, it’s obvious that the Hastings, especially Jessica, are responsible for integrating their socialist’s beliefs into the curriculum of all the government run public schools.

“Seems they started a test educational program several years ago. They took the best students, the cream of the crop, so to speak and kept them in a closed structured society for a period of six weeks with little or no communication with their families.

“I read actual reports from some of the students that attended those schools, and their comments are eye opening.

“They said that they were taught values that go totally against what this nation was founded on and were told to forget all the values that they grew up with and adhere to their new world teachings.

"They were further instructed to totally ignore their parents—to play as though they were listening to them, 'sucker them in' was how the one boy's report stated; this because parents wouldn't understand the children's superior thought process.

"Other than severing the parent-child relationship, these schools taught anti-Christian values, radical socialism, pacifism, and a consistent hostility toward Western civilization and culture.

"Reed, for years now this White House has been indoctrinating their anti-Constitutional and socialistic views into the minds of the children. They know that they control the future if they control the children.

"Isn't it ironic how we hear either the president or Jessica always pushing for better education programs, spouting their favorite catch phrase, 'it's about children; it's all for the children'?"

"I know, Kate, that some parents are aware of what's taking place, and they're either home teaching their children or sending them to private schools.

"But the majority of parents believe what the president and first lady say about their desire to make the education system better in academic standards and these are the ones that fall in with the rest of the uninformed flock, while the president continues adding rungs to his ladder, edging ever nearer to total control over our country and it's people. If only the people would just take time; it's all out there for them to discover; the executive orders, Congressional Reports, Congressional Hearings; it's all available to the public."

Kate sighed and slowly nodded.

"Reed, I agree that some people out there are paying attention, and are aware that things aren't right, but still the majority of the country are without a clue and soon they may lose all of their Constitutional freedoms. This president has so much charisma that he has completely mesmerized the people as a whole. One thing is certain, if Hastings declares martial law, it won't be temporary. There is barely a trickle of news getting out to the public about anything that makes the administration look bad. Except for a few rogues like yourself, the rest of the press are mum on any underhanded activities. What's sad is the public doesn't pay attention when something does leak out into the mainstream media. Reed, I'll do whatever I can to try to help you and the general out, so you can count me in for the duration."

"Thank you, the general was sure that you would go for it, and I'm happy to have you fighting the fight with us."

Looking at the time, Reed said he should be going and Kate rose to get his coat. As he walked toward to door with Kate's papers in hand, he thanked her, and with a slight kiss on her cheek, told her to be careful.

"I'll phone you in the next couple of days. Good night, Kat," and then was out the door.

Leaning against the closed door, Kate smiled and thought how she had always disliked being called Kat, but admitted that she liked the soft way it had flowed from Reed's lips.

Chapter 4

The following day found Kate extremely busy. The stock market was holding steady, but the public remained jittery, and were looking for solutions to save their invested earnings.

Frank Oliver, the head of the Federal Reserve, had gone on television early in the morning, and laid out his plan to get the market headed in an upward trend. His expertise was well regarded by the general public, and he allayed the swell of panic in the land, at least for the time being.

However, another crisis had cropped up.

Three months ago, the president had issued an executive order stating that every gun owner in the country must register their weapons with the Federal Government.

During the last month, the National Rifle Association had been appearing on talk shows across the country, trying to get the word out to defeat the order. They were saying that the law-abiding citizens would be the only ones to obey and register their arms, and that the criminal element, who acquire their weapons illegally, would never register. They argued that the second amendment to the Constitution states "a well-regulated militia being necessary to the security of a free state, the right of the people to keep and bear arms shall not be infringed." Their fear was that if the Government had ready access to all registered weapons, they could confiscate them at their will.

The advocates of the gun law were touting their own reasons for wanting the registration to take place. They believed that it would indeed deter crime and accidents related to guns, though they never could give any valid reasons how the registration of arms could determine how those arms would be used. How they intended to get the criminals to register weapons was somewhat obscure.

On and on the arguments waged, and in the end, because the Congress was so divided on the issue, they never even brought it to a vote. Time just ran out on them, for they had only ninety days in which to accept it or reject it. Now, it had become law, just as so many other executive orders had done.

The administration immediately issued a news release to the public saying that each and every gun owner must have their weapons registered by December thirty-first, nineteen hundred ninety-nine.

Because of the uproar, Kate had been ordered to field all calls. Betts said that he would take calls only from the president, Hargraves, Hicks, or Preston. All others were to be given a statement which he prepared and gave to Kate for response. Call after call from senators, representatives and the press were met with this same message.

"It is a red-letter day for the good citizens of the country. The gun law is a major step toward gun control and fighting crime. The president is pleased and has everything in place to make sure that this law is carried out to the letter. He promises it will all be for the good of the nation, and it will be accomplished by months' end."

As busy as she was giving her prepared speech, Kate was fortunate enough to catch part of Betts conversation with the attorney general.

With her intercom open, she listened to Betts saying to Hargraves "John, this is a big one for us. I didn't think the president could pull it off. Everything is sliding into place, and when the time comes, it's going to be a roll-over. The bird-brained public out there thinks the president ought to have a medal, for crying out loud; what a total bunch of idiots. Some of them even think that the criminals are going to wander in and happily register their illegal weapons. But these are the people who voted our Will into office twice. Hah! I tell you John, Hastings has the citizens of this country so brainwashed they've forgotten how to think rationally."

Kate spotted a shadow approaching her office door window and quickly flipped off the intercom key.

Pretending to type, she looked up as the door opened to admit General Manning.

"Is Jason busy? It's important that I speak to him."

Kate buzzed the inner office and announced the general and was quickly told to send him right in.

"Mr. Betts says for you to go right in, General," and before she finished speaking, he had gone through the door and closed it behind him.

Beside herself with wanting to find out what they were conversing about, she was exasperated when Gail came bursting through the door.

"Wow! What a day. Have your phones been busy?"

Without waiting for an answer she went on.

"Mine have been blowing their buttons, and all over some little gun registration law....go figure. Anyway, I just dropped in to tell you that I won't be in tomorrow. My boss says he has something scheduled and so gave me the day off. With a three day weekend, I'm flying to Atlantic City with Ken. He's that hunk I told you about. I've been seeing a lot of him lately. Gosh, Kate, you look really frazzled. Obviously you could use a day off yourself. Well, cheer up, it's about time to leave and put it all behind you. See ya next week," and with her usual flurry, out the door she went.

There wasn't a chance for Kate to respond even if she had wanted to.

Happy that she was finally alone, she immediately flipped the intercom key. The general was speaking.

"...snooping around the Control Center. There's good reason to believe that he was reporting to the first lady. We had to eliminate him. The men are busy now setting it up to look like a suicide. We don't know how many more moles she has planted about, but what we do know is that the first lady has her own agenda. She has these grandiose aspirations of running for president herself come two thousand four. She's been hitting on all burners, working this country, telling the people everything they want to hear, and they're snatching up every bone she tosses them. None of the numskull masses even have a clue that it's all one big act. Up till now the president has given her free rein to keep her out of his way, but now she's become suspicious of Will and has spies everywhere. She's not going to put up with anything ruining her presidential push."

"You're not telling me anything I didn't already know about Jessica," Betts broke in. "What I do want to know is how much of the president's plan has his wife found out about. You'd better finish up with that Secret Service mole. Make sure that it does look like a suicide. We can't afford any foul-ups at this stage. I'll get with Will and get this problem of his wife resolved, and quickly."

Kate sensed an end to the conversation and quietly flicked the intercom off.

Sitting, shuffling folders around to look like she was cleaning off her desk for the day, she just had time to glance up to see the general disappear out her door.

Mr. Betts came out shortly to announce his departure and told Kate there were two files on his desk he wanted her to take care of, then she was free to leave for the day.

He was gone before she could say good night. Just as well. She couldn't trust her voice to be calm after hearing the two men discussing a murder as though it were an everyday occurrence.

"My good Lord," she thought, "what kind of maniacs have we got running this country."

Trying as best she could to bring herself under control, she got her work cleaned up in record time and made a beeline for home.

Once there, she quickly sat down and made notes of Manning and Betts' conversation, and what Betts had said to Hargraves on the phone. That done, she put her dinner on to cook and went to the bedroom to change clothes. The doorbell rang and answering it, she found Diane standing there.

"C'mon in," Kate greeted her and led the way into the kitchen.

"What's going on, girlfriend? Mom tells me you had Reed over for dinner last night. Is this the beginning of something I should know about?"

Kate grinned coyly and continued filling up a couple glasses of wine.

"It was just a friendly gesture to thank Reed for seeing me home the other night, nothing more. Although I do admit that there is a definite attraction there and I wouldn't mind seeing more of Mr. Adams." She checked her dinner and continued on. "He's invited me to dinner at his place, but no set date yet. I like him and I'm hoping that the feeling is mutual. Now that you've found out what you dropped in for," Kate said with a laugh, "what's new with you and Joe?"

Diane filled her in on the latest news while Kate finished her cooking. Noticing that the food was ready, Diane said that it was time for her to get going.

"Enjoy your dinner. Oh, and don't forget Reed's talk show is on tonight," she said making her way to the door.

"Thanks, Diane, for reminding me. I'd planned to watch."

Seeing her friend out the door, she closed and bolted it, then went in to have dinner. After eating her fill, she cleaned up the kitchen, went into the den and turned on the television. While she waited for the program to start, she wondered if she should phone Reed later with her news or wait until he phoned her the next day. She decided that her news was important enough for her to contact him after the program.

She glanced up and heard Reed introducing his four guests. The discussion tonight was on the gun registration. His guests were a representative from the National Rifle Association, a Mr. Dan Rivers, two senators, one from each party, Senator Defoe from Arkansas and Senator Herrick from New York. The other was Andy Eldridge, a columnist for *The Los Angeles Times*.

Back and forth they went, the advocates pushing their views with the same old White House cliches and spin, and the opposers trying to make their point that it was indeed an infringement of the right for people to bear arms.

They concluded with their summaries, and Reed finished up with his predictions of more government control. He warned the public not to be complacent when their Constitutional rights were being infringed upon.

Announcing his topic for next week's program, Reed said good night to his viewing audience and the show ended.

Kate checked the phone book for the number at the station and dialed. When someone answered, she asked if Mr. Adams was still there. She was asked to hold while they checked. In a few minutes she heard Reed's voice on the other end of the line.

"Reed, this is Kate. I have some news I think will be of interest to you."

She got no further before Reed broke in.

"I'll be there in a half hour. Have my drink ready."

"Will do, see you then," and she heard the line click dead.

Arriving sooner than expected, the doorbell caught Kate in the bedroom giving her hair a quick brush and dabbing on a touch of lipstick. She made a dash for the door, opened it, and ushered him in.

Reed threw his coat over the back of a chair and followed Kate to the kitchen. Gathering up their drinks, they went into the den and both sat down on the couch.

"Why the urgency, Kat, what have you found out?"

Taken back for a moment when he called her Kat again, she quickly jumped up, excused herself, and went to get her notes. On the way she told herself not to allow him to discombobulate her senses. He affected her in the craziest way, and she was sure that he was well aware of that fact.

Her resolve in place once again, she came back and plopped down beside him and handed over the notes she had made of Betts conversations with Hargraves and Manning.

Reed was intent and Kate could see his eyes growing dark. When he finished, he looked up and met her eyes.

"Kat, do you have any idea of what's behind this?"

"Just that they have murdered someone in cold blood who they think was spying for the first lady," she replied with a questioning look.

"The general has men planted everywhere also, trying to ferret out information for us," Reed interjected. "This Secret Service man that met his untimely death, could very well be one of ours. No one suspected you of overhearing this diatribe, did they?"

"No, there was absolutely no problem along that line," she assured him.

"It looks to me like the first lady is in way over her head on this one," he ventured. "If she is known by the president and his ghoulies to have plants in their midst, her life isn't worth a plug nickel. Ironically, they think it was her man they nailed, though we can't be sure that it wasn't. I'm just sorry that you didn't start your eavesdropping much sooner. However, I forbid you to take any rash actions that could very well put you in danger. You've witnessed how they treat any interlopers. Promise me that you'll take every precaution to protect yourself."

"I'll do what I can, Reed. I don't proclaim to be anything but truly frightened, and the truth be known, I'm looking forward to a future life for myself before casting off these mortal bonds."

"I'd like very much to stay longer, but I've got to get these notes over to the general. Are you free tomorrow night? I'm open if you'd like to try that dinner I promised you."

"I'd be delighted to have dinner with you, but I haven't a clue to where you live. Let me get a piece of paper and you can write down the address and any directions you think I might need."

Reed jotted down the information, including his private cell phone number, and said that by tomorrow night they should know if the slain man was one of theirs.

He stood up and retrieved his coat. As they made their way to the door, he reached out and took her hand in his.

"I'll be looking forward to seeing you tomorrow, and I promise you that all this talk of intrigue will be put on the back burner. It'll just be you and me, Kat, enjoying each other, along with good food, good wine and a warm fire to cozy up to."

"I'd like that very much. It sounds like a lovely evening. What time would you like me there?"

"How about seven? You don't have to work Saturday, do you?"

"Never on Saturday. That's taboo here in D.C.," she laughed.

As they stood at the door, Reed let go of her hand and pulled her to him. He lifted her chin up slightly and kissed her softly on the lips. Raising back, their eyes met, then their lips met once again with a more urgent, deeper need.

When at last they broke free, Kate could feel her face flushed and as she held Reed's gaze, she could see the passion in his darkening eyes.

"I'll see you at seven, my sweet Kat."

And as he went out the door, she murmured a soft "Good night, Reed."

Chapter 5

Friday, and the calm was almost deafening compared to yesterday's whirlwind of activity around the office. Hicks, the press secretary, stopped in for updates on the Chinese acquisition of United States nuclear technology. The press was pushing to know if the administration was beefing up security at the nuclear laboratories, and why didn't the president take steps sooner when he first found out that technology was being pilfered.

Betts had earlier dictated to Kate the usual statements on the matter, filled with double-talk and misleading phrases, placing the blame on others.

She also handed Hicks the prepared statement on the gun registration that was now in effect, saying that the president was happy with the speedy actions taking place in compliance with the new law.

With no other pressing matters, she phoned Diane and they met at their usual restaurant to have lunch and catch up on each other's news. Diane was excited to hear of Kate's dinner with Reed and told her, as they were leaving, she wanted to hear all about it, and would drop by on Sunday.

Back at the office, Kate spotted a note on her desk saying that Betts had a lengthy meeting that afternoon and that when her work was completed, she was free to leave for the weekend.

Kate wondered what meeting had come up. She knew of none. Instantly becoming suspicious, she made her way into Betts' office and straightened his desk while looking for some clue as to where he might have gone. She noticed the pad by his telephone and could see little indentations left from something he had written down. She quickly reached for a pencil and very lightly went over the pad, revealing the words "Genesis, one."

"There's that name again," she thought, and tearing off the paper, she stuck it in her pocket.

As she finished up her work, she couldn't help but wonder once again what it could refer to and why she never heard it mentioned by Betts. She must remember to ask Reed about it tonight and see if it rings a bell with him.

Off in a securely guarded room underneath the Pentagon, five men grouped around a table. Genesis was in motion.

The president addressed the others one at a time.

"Hargraves, is everything moving along with the gun registration?"

"Ahead of schedule, Mr. President. We should have one hundred percent registration well before the deadline."

"Good. Preston, how are you coming with setting up the Troops? I want the National Guard and FEMA set up in every city around the country. We'll need them out in the streets within minutes of zero hour. Make sure they know what to do, and what they're going to tell the good citizens," he added with a sneer.

"Everything is set in place, sir, and every unit commander has his orders. There'll be no hang-ups from our end."

"Thank you, Mike, I knew you were the one to undertake this job. General, is all in readiness at the Missile Launch Center? There can be no slip-ups from that quarter. Check and recheck every mechanism. If anything goes awry there, the rest is so much water under the bridge."

"Everything's working fine, Mr. President. There's nothing amiss and no one suspects anything out of the ordinary. The others that have access to the bunker are unable to detect anything different. The missiles are in readiness at all times, as is our general policy, so nothing is suspect to probing eyes. I do want to add, sir, that the person we eliminated yesterday was one of your wife's plants. We can't take a chance with anyone poking around in there. Someone smart enough could take note of the coordinates, and we can't have that."

"Okay, Tim, you're right to eliminate anyone caught snooping around. All precautions must be taken at your post. Jason, last but not least, have you got the press, media, and the citizens under control? They must remain in the dark until after the fact, then it will be of no consequence. We have ninety percent of the press and media in our corner, but they're starting to have qualms about things such as their beloved armed forces losing their lives in foreign countries, the failing economy, stock market crash and such. You have to keep them pacified a little longer, Betts. Think you can do that?"

"It's getting a little sticky, Will. The citizens and even our White House controlled press don't like it when their soldiers die in battles of a questionable nature. There's a lot of dissension on the Macedonia aggression. Usually our press loves wars, in fact, they thrive on it; but the people are giving them such a bad time that they're having to act like they're concerned. They're playing the game right along with us. It's the rogue reporters that have to be kept in check, and they can be put off till after the new year."

"Make sure you do, Jason. We don't want any uprisings to deal with. I needed to dwindle the forces here at home, and that was a made-to-order setup to get rid of them. Couldn't leave any chance for the military getting involved here at home. Well, men, it looks as if everything is moving with ease. Does anyone have anything to add, or any questions?"

"Just a reminder, Will, that something has to be done to curb Jessica's probing," Betts stated.

"That will be resolved before long," the president finished. "All right then, it looks as if our "Rebirth" is beginning. If there's nothing further, I suggest we adjourn and enjoy our weekend."

With that, the five rose and left the room.

Back at the office, Kate had finished her work, closed up shop and headed out the door. Presenting her pass to Jim, she wished him a good weekend and was on her way.

She had a few stops to make, first for gas, which was at an all time high of two dollars and twenty cents a gallon, then on to the mall. There she purchased some of her favorite cologne, which she was out of, and skipped by the jewelry shop to have them put a new battery in her watch.

Reaching home, she kicked off her shoes and poured herself a glass of wine. She sat down, put her feet up and took a relaxing sip. Planning what she would wear and wondering what this night would bring brought a pleasant smile to her lips. She remembered the note in her pocket, took it out, and put it in the purse she was going to take with her to Reed's.

As she glanced out the window, she saw that it was threatening snow. She had heard a forecast, and they had predicted snow for that night and the next morning. It made her realize that Christmas was not far off and she still had shopping to do.

She loved this time of year with all the hustling and bustling crowds. It brought to mind her grandparent's place in the country and how beautiful it looked with the fresh fallen snow. She must give them a call and let them know to expect her for Christmas, and she made a mental note to do that over the weekend.

Shaking herself out of her reverie, she looked up at the wall clock and saw that it was time to get showered and dressed.

She ambled into the bedroom, undressed, and went in to turn on the shower. A short time later she was at her dressing table in her lacy underwear, blow-drying her hair. She left it down and flowing in her usual casual style. Going to her closet, she pulled out her pale yellow wool slacks and a creamy silk, tailored long-sleeve blouse. She tucked her blouse in her slacks and slipped into a pair of darker gold flats.

Satisfied and comfortable with her look, she donned her coat, put on her gloves, then went into the other room and picked up her purse and keys. A quick look around, and she was out the door on her way.

She had no trouble finding the streets that Reed had instructed her to take and soon found herself on the street where he lived. She had a strange feeling of déjà vu as she drove slowly checking addresses.

"Odd," she thought, "I've never been in this area of town before, but it seems rather familiar."

Spotting his apartment house, she slowed to a stop and parked. It had begun to snow lightly, and as she got out and locked her door, she looked up to catch a few snow flakes on her tongue. Walking up the steps, she felt her heart beat faster and chided herself for feeling like a teenager that had a crush for the first time. She found Reed's apartment number and knocked gingerly.

No sooner done than the door swung open, and there stood her gallant host. She thought that he was even more handsome tonight with his casual look in a pair of snug fitting levis and an off-white bulky pullover sweater. He waved with a flourish and stepped aside to let her enter. He took her coat and purse and put them in a nearby closet. Coming back to her, he gave her a soft kiss and put an arm around her waist to lead her into the living room.

"Oh, Reed, what a lovely home," she exclaimed. "Everything is so tasteful and comfortable looking."

Her eyes wandered around the room taking in everything from the paintings on the wall to the inviting roaring fire in the huge brick fireplace.

"Come out to the kitchen with me and I'll fix our drinks, then we'll take the grand tour."

A few minutes later, with their drinks in hand, he showed her around the rest of the apartment. His den also had a fireplace aglow with a warm fire. On the mantle there were several awards that he had acquired for outstanding journalism through the years. The bedrooms were large and done in beautiful colors and decor.

Steering her back toward the den he asked, "Would you prefer the living room or the den to sit?"

"The living room is elegant, Reed, but let's sit in here. It's so warm and comfortable looking and you have a great view of the snow falling outside."

"Done," he stated, as he led her over to a large pillowy soft couch. "By the way, Kat, I have to give most of the decorating credit to my sister Jean. She was kind enough to come down from Philadelphia and take charge. She did a great job, and knew what I liked, and I'm very comfortable here. It's also quite handy to the station, and I have a nice, quiet den to write my columns, which I just fax in to the paper."

As they sat enjoying each other's company and sipping their drinks, they noticed that the snow was getting heavier.

"What a beautiful snow fall," she murmured and walked over to the window for a closer look out at the street below.

Reed followed her over and put his arm around her. They stood quietly in their own thoughts watching the huge flakes fall past the window to the snow-covered ground.

Reed broke the silence. "I'd better get out to the kitchen and tend to our dinner. Would you like to keep the chef company?"

"I've been smelling a delicious aroma wafting from there and now's my chance to see what the source is. Is there anything I can do to help?"

"You can help by just giving me something beautiful to look at as I work," he grinned.

Kate enjoyed watching him as he finished preparing the meal and put it into serving dishes. She thought how very seductive he looked with his dark blond hair a bit mussed. When he turned to her, she detected just the slightest hint of a dimple as he grinned and said, "Roast beef stroganoff for milady, with wild rice, broccoli au gratin, and for dessert, custard flan."

Kate laughed. "It's truly a meal fit for royalty. You certainly aren't lacking in cooking skills."

He filled a couple of goblets with a rosé wine, and they sat down to eat. The table was set with style. In the center was placed a shallow bowl with pale yellow roses floating gently on the water. Several thin, pale yellow candles surrounded the bowl, flickering soft light over the tempting plates of food.

Kate noted that he once again set their places side-by-side.

"As you may have guessed, Kat, I don't like sitting at opposite ends of a table. Too much of a formal, cold feeling about it."

"I have been wondering about it, and I have to say that I agree with your reasoning."

They sat quietly chatting while savoring the flavorful meal.

"Reed, do you know of any place or any thing in the area called Genesis?

He gave a thoughtful look and after a minute stated that he knew of nothing by that name.

"I know you don't want to talk shop tonight, but this has been nagging at me. I found a note on Betts' desk last week and it had '"Genesis, meeting, nine.' Then, just today, he left a note on my desk while I was out to lunch. It said he had a lengthy meeting to attend this afternoon. While cleaning up his desk, I noticed something had been written on his phone pad, and when I ran a pencil lightly over it, "Genesis, one," appeared. I have the note in my purse if you'd like to look at it later. Why I question it is because I schedule all his meetings, but he seems to want to keep this Genesis to himself."

"It does have some undertones to it," Reed replied. "It may be nothing, but it sounds valid enough to demand further investigation, so continue to keep your eyes and ears open about it. I'll take a look at it later. You're right to tell me anything and everything that you think is the least suspicious. Everything helps to fit the pieces together.

"But for now, we'll forget that there's anything evil going on. C'mon, finish your dessert. When you're done I'll get these dishes cleaned off and straighten up the kitchen, then we can relax by the fire."

"This meal was delicious, Reed, and the flan was sumptuous," she exclaimed.

They rose from the table and she helped him clean up. They laughed and joked away as they did their work.

When finished, Kate made her way into the den, kicked off her shoes and curled up on the couch in front of the fire.

Reed followed shortly with their after-dinner drinks in hand. He set them down on the table in front of the couch and went over to add some big logs to the waning fire, and soon it roared to life again.

He came back and sat down beside her and handed her drink over. He reached down and took a sip of his, then replaced it. Kate did the same. Sitting back, Reed put his arm around Kate and pulled her close. She didn't hold back and snuggled in closer, laying her head against his chest. It felt right being here in his arms and she was feeling strong stirrings of desire from the nearness of him.

Reed was also feeling the attraction and knew that he cared for this woman in a deep, intimate way.

"You've completely taken me off guard, Kat. I've hardly been able to keep my wits about me since I laid eyes on you. You're so distractingly beautiful with that soft brown hair and those green, cat eyes. I'm afraid I've fallen head over heels for you, Kat, my love."

She lifted her head and gazed into his eyes.

"Oh, Reed, I feel the same way. Do you think we're out of our minds? I mean, we've only just gotten to know one another. My heart tells me that it doesn't matter, but my brain is saying, "Hold on there, girl.'"

"Look, my love," he said softly, "time is not important when every part of you says it's right. Go with your heart Kat, and leave the rest to sort itself out."

He pulled her close and gave her a long, deep kiss. Breaking apart, he held her tightly, and they could feel the beat of their hearts in rapid unison.

"Kat, stay with me tonight."

"Yes Reed, I want to, and there's no sense denying it. I want you to make love to me and I want to fall asleep with your arms wrapped around me."

"Ah, my sweet, Kat, you're so beautiful, so warm. We shall see if this night brings much sleep," he whispered.

With the snow falling and the fire waning, he slid his arms underneath her, lifted her up and carried her into his bedroom.

Chapter 6

In the wee small hours of the morning a battle royal was taking place in the president's quarters of the White House.

The president confronted the first lady about her planted spies.

"I know all about your little subterfuge, my dear Jessica. I have no idea what you think to accomplish by this stupidity. Just what is it you think is going on?"

"I know that you're plotting something," Jessica sneered, "and I know that whatever it is, it's going to happen soon."

"You've gone too far, Jessica. You'd better back off and call off your moles before they all get themselves killed, and do it fast," he yelled.

"You're ruining everything, you idiot," she screamed at him. "We had an agreement when we set out to gain the White House that you would serve your terms, then I would run for president. I've been working the people of this country for years, and I've succeeded in making them believe that I'm their "Mother Benefactor." The time will be ripe for me to run in two thousand four. I've got them lapping up every piece of garbage I throw at them. I'll be a shoe-in, Will, and you're not going to ruin my hard work! I've been traveling to every country on the globe, ingratiating myself to all their heads of state. All these years of so-called good will tours spouting unity, human rights and women's rights. I want to throw up from all the syrupy speeches I have to give. I've fooled them all, Will, just as you have. With all that I've had to endure, I deserve my day on the throne, and I'm going to get it! You're not going to screw it up for me," she shrieked. "I already know when you plan your little coup de grâce, and if you don't stop this charade at once, I swear I'll leak it to the press." Not a bad idea considering I'd be the poor, innocent first lady. And you can bet I'll play it to the hilt. Every sap in the country will feel sorry for me."

"You won't do anything, Jessica, because you have nothing to leak, you bitch! You're blowing hot air as usual."

"We'll just see what I have, and if I lose one more of my men, I will blow the lid off anything you've got planned!"

On and on it went, voices gaining more volume with each passing minute. A couple of Secret Service men were in easy hearing and could hear Jessica screaming like a banshee, spewing out four-letter words that would make a stevedore blush.

The president held his own, roaring like a raving maniac. After a couple of hours of this clamor, things started to quiet down.

"You just keep out of my sight, Jessica, and call off your detectives, or I won't be responsible."

"I'll keep out of your sight, all right, but if you think that I'll give up on thwarting whatever it is you've got in mind, think again, Will. I intend to have my day, and you'd better believe that I mean to get it! And you won't have to see my face again until the gala on Thursday."

The nation's first couple hated one another, but had no trouble acting the loving couple in public and in front of the television cameras. After so many years, they were experts in covering up their true feelings for one another.

A short time later, the president sat in his office contemplating his dilemma with his wife. He sat up and placed a call on his private phone. In quiet tones he put a plan in motion.

"I want no slipups, is that understood? This must be clean and untraceable. Her plane takes off at three o'clock on Friday. She's flying to Tennessee to spend Christmas with her mother. I've already told her that I'd fly in later that night after I tend to some things here. Make sure her plane never gets there. When it's done, contact me immediately."

He hung up the phone and sat quietly for a few minutes, then leaned back and lit up a cigar.

A different scene was taking place across town. Reed and Kate had just finished a tasty breakfast he had prepared for the two of them.

"Kat, I'm sorry you have to leave soon. I'd like you to stay the weekend. I know, I know, you've already told me about your busy schedule, but I'm not one to give up easily. Having you here with me makes me just want more of you."

"There's absolutely nothing I'd enjoy more than staying with you, Reed. What we shared last night was something I've only dreamed about. Maybe when all this intrigue is over, we'll have all the time in the world to pursue out relationship."

"I'm hoping for that, and soon," he whispered in her ear as he brushed by on the way to the sink.

Just then the phone rang and Reed reached over and picked up the receiver.

"Hello."

"Hello, Reed, this is Brad. I just got word that the man who was killed the other day is not one of ours. They're saying it was a suicide. I thought you'd like to know."

"Thanks, general, Jessica's not going to be happy about this when she finds out. Is there anything else happening?"

"Nothing breaking, but there are a few details I'd like to go over with you, if you can get by over the weekend."

"I'm free this afternoon, if that suits you, general."

Agreeing to a time, Reed then asked him if he had ever come across the name Genesis. He responded in the negative, and Reed went on to tell him what Kate had revealed to him.

"I'll keep my ears open, Reed, and give Kate my best when you see her."

They said their good-byes and Reed set the phone back in its holder. While he had been talking, Kate had gone to get her purse and dug out the note. She had it on the table, and Reed picked it up to study it. While doing so, he told her about the dead man.

"Go ahead and keep the note, Reed. I have no use for it. And now, I must be going. I promised myself that I'd complete my Christmas shopping today, and I have a lot to do. I have to call my grandparents, too, and let them know that I'll be coming for Christmas. It's almost upon us. The presidential gala is on the twenty-third, and I plan to leave the next day for home."

"I didn't know you'd be attending the gala, Kat. I'll be there, covering it for my paper. We'll have to act like strangers if we should run into one another."

"The Powers are going. Perhaps if you spoke to them about our problem, they could pretend to introduce us. What do you think?"

"That ought to work. It would allow us to converse without drawing suspicious glances," Reed grinned.

"And now, I'm on my way to a big day of shopping. Reed, last night is something that I shall remember and hold in my heart. Thank you for giving it to me."

"It's I who'll savor the memory, my sweet Kat. I predict that we'll have many, more such nights."

Putting his arm around her waist, he walked her into the hallway where he retrieved her coat from the closet and helped her on with it. Taking her in his arms, he gave her a lingering kiss. Kate broke free, flushed, and told Reed good-bye.

"Good-bye, Kat, my love."

Arriving home to change her clothes, Kate picked up her paper and flipped through it looking over the Christmas sales, then headed for the bedroom to change clothes.

Soon she was on her way to the mall. She spent all afternoon making purchases for each person on her list. She thought that she would like to buy something for Reed, but didn't have a clue to what he might like.

She bought a cup of coffee at a little cafe and sat down at one of their outside tables. She went over different things in her mind and finally decided on a sweater.

That done, she finished her coffee and started for the men's shop she remembered passing on her way to the cafe. She sorted through piles of sweaters and opted for a wheat-colored cable knit.

With all her purchases in tow, she made one last stop to buy wrapping and ribbon. Weaving her way through the crowds she found her way back to her car. Piling all her packages in the back seat, she headed for home.

After dinner she placed a phone call to her grandparents.

"Hi, Gram, how are you?"

"Kate, honey, it's so good to hear your voice. Both Gramps and I are fine."

"Did you get any snow from that front moving through?" Kate questioned.

"Yes, dear, we have about a foot on the ground and piled higher where the drifts are. The countryside looks beautiful, and Gramps was lucky to get the outside lights up just before the storm hit. How have you been, dear, is everything going well?"

"Everything's fine, Gram. I'm calling to let you know that I'll be coming home for Christmas. I'll be flying in on Friday and will return Sunday."

"Oh, Kate, that's wonderful. It will be so good to have you home."

"Gram, I've met a very special man, and I can't wait to tell you about him when I get there."

"Sounds pretty serious, Kate. It's about time you found someone. Why don't you invite him to come with you? We'd love to meet him and there's plenty of room."

"I don't know, Gram. He has a large family and may have already made plans to spend Christmas with them. But I'll ask him and see if he might be free."

"Please do that, dear, we'd be so happy to meet him."

"Can I speak to Gramps for a minute before I hang up?"

"He's right here. He's been listening on the other phone. I'll say good-bye, dear, and hang up so you two can talk."

"G'bye, Gram."

"Hello, Kate, I didn't want to barge in on your talk with Gram. What time can we expect you Friday? Do you want me to pick you up at the airport?"

"Yes, Gramps, I'd like you to come get me. There's no sense renting a car just for two days. Besides, you have an extra car if I need one. I'll be getting in at three forty-five in the afternoon. Hopefully, there won't be any delays because of bad weather. I'll be flying US Air, flight number four twenty-six."

"Okay, I've got it all written down. I'll call the airport before I leave to make sure your flight took off on time. We're expecting more snow for Christmas, so it should be a pretty one here this year."

"It sounds lovely, Gramps. I'd better go now. I love you, and tell Gram I love her too. I'll see you both on Friday."

"G'bye, Kate, we love you."

Pouring herself a cup of coffee, she set about wrapping gifts. It took her the rest of the evening to finish and get the extra wrappings put away. Tomorrow she would put up her small tree.

Tired from her long day, she grabbed a quick snack, then went in to shower. Climbing into bed, she pulled the blanket up just as the phone jangled.

"Hello."

"Hello, Kat, just calling to wish you sweet dreams."

"Thank you, Reed, and I wish you the same."

"Did you get all your shopping finished?"

"Yes, and what a day it was. Reed, I phoned my grandparents to let them know when to expect me, and they issued an invitation to you to spend the holiday with us. I told them you probably had family plans, but that I would ask."

"Kat, I would love to go with you! I've been racking my brain trying to come up with some way to spend Christmas with you. I can see my family anytime. We can't be seen together here, and your grandparents' country home is the perfect solution to spending time together. Will you tell them that I wholeheartedly accept their invitation?"

"I will," Kate said with a laugh.

"By the way, just where is it we're going? All you've told me is that they have a country place in upstate New York."

First, she gave him the name of the airlines, the flight number, time and destination.

"The closest city is Elmira, which is just about on the New York-Pennsylvania border. The countryside is the most beautiful I've ever seen."

"It sounds perfect, Kat. And now I had better let you get to sleep. I'll be looking forward to spending the holiday with you. G'nite, my love."

"G'nite, Reed."

A bright sunny morning found Kate on her weekly jog. She thought how calm and peaceful everything seemed. The sun was glistening on the snow, forming millions of tiny rainbows on its surface.

How the calm belied the undercurrent of events taking place. Would they be able to abort the plans of the president, she wondered. She assembled the facts in her mind and tried to come up with some plan of her own.

"There has to be something in Betts' office that will give me insight as to what they have planned," she mused, "but what and where to find it."

Resolving to do some snooping around in the next few days, Kate turned onto her street and hopped up the steps to her apartment.

She changed from her sweats into some comfortable Levis and a tee shirt, fixed herself a cup of hot chocolate, and sat down to read the Sunday paper.

News of more American casualties in Macedonia headlined the front page.

She browsed through the letters to the editor, and found many that were unhappy with the war, gun registration, high gas prices, and the general state of the economy.

She spotted an article on the upcoming Belkhanov visit on Thursday, and all that was planned by the White House.

Further on there was a short paragraph telling of the first family's holiday plans. It stated that the first lady would fly to Tennessee on Friday to spend the weekend with her mother and that the president planned to join them later.

"Looks like I'm not the only one leaving town for the holiday," she mused.

Putting the newspaper aside, she went to the storage closet, pulled out a large box and several smaller boxes and put them in the den. The next several hours were spent setting up her tree and decorating it.

She added a few garlands of holly and other decorative things around the apartment. Finishing it off, she hung on her front door a huge live wreath she had picked up at a Christmas tree lot . Happy with her efforts, she put the empty boxes away and vacuumed up the loose tinsel that had scattered around the floor. She piled her gifts under the tree and went in to fix herself something to eat.

As she was packing the dishwasher, the doorbell rang, and answering it, she found Diane waiting. Zipping past, she was almost to the kitchen before Kate got the door shut and bolted.

"Fill me in, Kate, how did your date with Reed go? Did you two hit it off? Are you going to see him again?"

"Whoa, hold on," Kate said laughing. "Let me pour us a drink and we'll go into the den. I need to get my feet up."

Making themselves comfortable, Diane remarked on how pretty the holiday decorations looked.

"Now, please, don't keep me in suspense any longer. I want all the details."

"Well," Kate began, "he fixed a superb dinner, and he's a gracious host. There were roaring fires in both fireplaces."

"All right, Kate," Diane broke in, "get to the important stuff."

"It was the most wonderful night of my life," she grinned. "I've fallen hook, line, and sinker, and I think he feels the same way. I stayed the night with him, Diane."

"Wow! Talk about fast, but I sensed there was something burning between you two at my parents' house. That wasn't animosity I saw in the looks you two were exchanging. Oh, Kate, I'm so happy for you! I only wish we had gotten you two together long ago."

"He's going with me to my grandparents for Christmas. It will give us a chance to spend some quality time together. We have so much to find out about each other."

"That'll be perfect! Wait till I tell my parents. They've been worried about his hermit-style life—all work and no play."

For another half hour the two friends chatted happily about their coming holiday plans. Finally, Diane got up, stretched and said she had to get going. Kate saw her to the door where they wished each other a good night.

Turning out the lights, Kate went in to shower, and watched a bit of television before retiring for the night.

Chapter 7

Kate was trying to shake off her nightmare. It was a repeat of her bone-chilling chase.

"Odd," she thought, the streets seem more familiar to me, most likely because I've seen them in three dreams now........wait a minute........I recognize the one street now," she exclaimed aloud. "It's the street Reed lives on! I must be trying to get to him. There must be something in the briefcase of importance. At least I have a start on solving this nightmare. I suspect the rest will follow in good time."

Noting the time she jumped out of bed, leaving the dilemma till another time. She was running late and chided herself for having to race around at the last minute.

Before long her day got under way, and soon she was on her way to the office. She got started with the usual preparation of documents that Betts would need that day.

Over at the general's home, two men conversed in private. Helene had already left for the University, and Brad was pouring Reed a cup of coffee. Reed spoke up.

"We've got to make more headway, and fast. I've been hearing more and more output by the White House in reference to terrorist threats that they have received from Jabar Murabi. They're pushing the idea that he's entered the country with a few of his Muslim friends. I'm trying to check it out. It's my belief that it's all White House spin to get their patsies lined up for their own cover-up. Have any of our people come up with anything helpful?"

"It's difficult, Reed, they have the lid buttoned down tight on this one. There's extra security roaming all over the bunker. Everyone still has access to everything, except the secret meeting room. My guess is they don't want to chance anyone slipping a bug in on them. It's as if it's a camouflage to throw off any suspicion as to what they're really planning. They know that Jessica's men are hovering around and it may be their way of distracting attention from the real plan. Reed, I can't believe that the president would take the disastrous risk of launching a nuclear missile. And where would he be aiming it? No, it just doesn't add up. Besides, all of us with coded passes are free to come and go into the Missile Launch Center. I thought I'd mosey in and take a look around to see if anything looks amiss."

Reed agreed, then added "Is there any way you can lay your hands on the blueprints for the Pentagon?"

"I should be able to get hold of them, but it'll take some doing. I can't promise to have them before next week. With the holiday coming up everything will be closed down."

"It won't give us much time, General, but maybe the blueprints will have an answer for us. They may give us a way to get in and bug that meeting room. If you find out anything new, contact me on my cell phone. But for now, I've got a column to write. I don't have to worry about my television show this week, they're preempting it so they can carry the gala live. Meantime, I'll do some digging around on my own and try to come up with something valid. So, I'll be on my way."

"I'll keep in touch, Reed, and let's hope something breaks soon."

The meeting over, they both went their separate ways for the day.

Back at the White House, preparations were under way for the Belkhanov visit. Protocol data was making it's rounds through the different offices.

The president and first lady were to greet Ivan Belkhanov and his wife Anna, at the South Portico entrance and proceed into the Blue Room for photo-ops. Kate spent the good part of the morning familiarizing herself with every detail. She wanted to make sure that she wouldn't be caught unaware and make some silly slipup.

Betts had already told her that she would sit at their table with him and his wife Caroline, Paul and Edith Robbins, John and Theresa Hargraves and Greg Hicks.

From dinner they were to proceed to the East Room, where there would be a reception line, with entertainment and dancing to follow.

Feeling comfortably sure that she had everything consigned to memory, Kate set the protocol aside and went to the cafeteria for some lunch.

Down at the Pentagon bunker, the general was taking the opportunity to venture into the Strategic Missile Launch Center. Since he was in charge until recently, there was no reason for concern among the guards. They saluted him as he slipped his code card into the slot that opened the door.

Once inside, he found himself alone, except for one engineer watching over the controls. Walking up to the man, who was a stranger to him, he casually asked how everything was going. He introduced himself and told him that this center was his charge until a few weeks ago.

The man introduced himself as Jeffrey Gobels. The general continued his conversation by asking a few personal questions of Gobels. He found out that he had recently been transferred to this post from the nuclear laboratory in New Mexico. His services had been personally requested by General Manning.

Saying he was going to take a look around before leaving, the general excused himself and wandered off.

He pretended to browse around the control panel showing little interest, while his keen eye scanned over the coordinates. Noting a change in one missile launch board, he tried to quickly note the change in his mind. Moving to other areas and supposedly acting interested, he ended up back where he started.

"Everything looks just as I left it, Jeffrey. Looks like you men are keeping it in shipshape order and ready to go. I sure miss my old command here, but that's the service for you. You go where they say."

"Ain't that the truth, General," Gobels put in. "I've been lucky though, having spent my entire career in the nuclear field."

"With those credentials, I don't doubt your expertise on the controls. They're fortunate to have acquired your services here. And now I must be getting back to my own matters. It's been very nice to meet you Gobels."

They shook hands, and the general made his departure.

Midafternoon found Kate typing up some memos for her boss when the door opened, and Gail came swooshing in.

"Hi, Kate, I just had to come by and tell you of my glorious trip to Atlantic City with Ken. What a time we had—dinners, shows, swimming, massages—you name it. Of course, we gambled some too. Ken is just so much fun, a real goer and doer, and he really likes me, Kate."

"I'm glad you enjoyed yourself, Gail. And I hope everything works out for you and Ken."

"Thanks, we've got a lot planned for the holidays too. You know we'll be shutting down Wednesday afternoon. Isn't that great? Four whole days off. Well, I gotta get back before the boss misses me. If I don't see you again before Wednesday, have a great Christmas!"

"You too, Gail," and the girl was gone in a flash. "What a whirlwind that girl is," Kate thought with a smile.

About four-thirty, a call came in for Betts from General Manning, which Kate put through. Being quiet, she listened on the intercom.

"I don't think we have to worry about Powers. It sounds from what you say, that he was just paying a nostalgic visit to his old command," she heard Betts say. "Gobels didn't detect any strange actions from the general. You said yourself nothing will look amiss to anyone snooping around. Yeah, I'll get with you later. There's a short meeting at the usual place on Thursday afternoon. The president has something he wants to tell us before we disburse for the holiday."

Kate flipped off the intercom and heard no more. She was busy cleaning up her desk when the inner door opened and Betts announced his departure. As soon as he left, she jotted down the one-sided conversation and pushed the paper into her purse.

Going into Betts' office, she did her clean-up and glanced around.

"There has to be something incriminating in here," she told herself as she wandered around his desk.

Pulling out one drawer after another, looking through the contents of each, she could find nothing out of the ordinary. Moving over to the file cabinets lined up against the wall, she checked each one. The ones that were familiar to her she passed by. In the second to the end cabinet she noticed the second drawer had no label. Reaching to click it open, she found it locked.

Going back to Betts' desk, she had just pulled out the middle drawer, when Betts himself came into the room.

"Mr. Betts, I thought you had left for the day," she said a little shakily having been surprised so suddenly.

Pretending to retrieve a couple of pencils from the drawer, she quickly shut it and moved to the pencil sharpener.

"I got all the way out to my car when I remembered something," he snapped, angry at having to make a return trip.

With an eye on her boss, she sharpened the pencils and turned back to place them on his desk. He opened the top right hand drawer and took out a ring with two keys on it. Kate put the pencils into a holder, looked around as though checking to see if she had done everything and then went toward the door.

Betts having gotten what he came after, gave her a darting look and was gone again.

Kate leaned on her desk and tried to quell her fear. Shaken by her close call, she took a minute to consider what had just taken place.

"I'm sure he didn't suspect me of anything. To him it looked as if I was just doing my routine work."

Satisfied that she wasn't suspect, she calmed down, picked up her things and left for home.

After dinner and a hot soak in the tub, Kate donned her favorite robe and went to pour herself some wine. She sat down in the den with her feet up under her and thought about what had transpired that day.

"Those keys must be important for Betts to have come back to retrieve them. One was small enough that it could be a file key but I have no idea what the larger one might fit. I must try to get hold of the one and see if it fits that drawer," she mused.

She finished her wine and went to get Reed's phone number. Dialing, she waited, and soon heard Reed's voice on the other end.

"Reed, this is Kate."

"Ah, Kat. What a pleasing end to a hectic day. Do I dare hope that you're calling because you miss me? Or do you have some information for me?"

"I do miss you, Reed, but I have something that I overheard today. It seems that General Powers was in the missile launch control room and it was reported to Manning. He phoned Betts to tell him. I think Manning may have been a little suspicious, but from what I heard on Betts' end, I don't think there's anything to worry about. Seems Betts believes the general was just paying a visit to his old stomping grounds. But Reed, I think that the general should know that his visit has been reported."

"You're right Kat, I'll inform the general tomorrow. I'll make him aware that he must take extra precautions. It's obvious they're getting antsy. Continue keeping your eyes and ears open, my sweet."

"I will, Reed."

She decided not to bring up her close call in Betts' office. Since there was no harm done, she wasn't going to worry Reed.

"Were you able to make your reservations for Friday?"

"Sure did, and there was no problem getting a seat on your flight. Seems there aren't many people traveling to that area over the holiday."

"You're probably right Reed, it's not a highly populated area—that's one of the reasons I love it so. I'm looking forward to going. It'll be good to get away from here".

"Possibly with clear minds we'll be able to make some sense out of all this when we get back," Reed added. "But most of all Kat, I'm going to just enjoy our time together."

"As will I. It's time to turn it in Reed, so I'll say g'nite."

"G'nite, my sweet, pleasant dreams."

The next day proved uneventful. Kate had little work to do with the holiday upon them. There were no pending meetings and nothing other than a few updates to give Hicks about the casualties in Macedonia.

"One thing for sure," Kate thought, "the troops over there are not resolving anything. Just more and more American lives being lost; and the majority of people are becoming angry with the president for taking this aggressive action."

The other thing Betts had given her to type up for Hicks was the latest rumors on Jabar Murabi, the Muslim terrorist. Supposedly the White House had been informed that there may be a bombing soon, but have not been able to determine where it is to happen. The report says that all security across the country should be beefed up and precautions taken.

Other than that, all other news for the press was coming out of the office directly involved with the Russian president's visit. So after Hicks picked up his press copies from Kate, Betts told her to go home.

Wednesday morning proved even more quiet with next to nothing to tend to.

There was a party in the early afternoon with punch and cookies and gifts for the workers sent down by the president and first lady.

In the aftermath of the party, Kate was gathering her things to leave for home when Betts came in and asked her to get the president on the line for him. After making the connection and putting it right through to Betts' office, Kate opened the intercom.

"Will, I won't hold you up, I wanted to let you know that I just got word about our nosy reporter, Reed Adams."

Kate inhaled sharply, held her breath, and prayed it wasn't bad news. She wished she could hear both ends of the conversation, but dared not lift the receiver.

"It seems that he's been poking his nose around talking to some of the Secret Service guys, asking them questions about the Pentagon and why we've felt it necessary to double security there. They all were prepared for those kind of questions, so there was no problem, since they've all been told that it's to protect against terrorist attacks. But, Will, I don't like this guy, he's like a bad nightmare; you wake up and he's still there. I've had him checked out and found out he's leaving town for the holiday, but I intend to have him watched when he gets back, just as a precaution. It's nice to know where your enemies are.

Yes, Will, I know what you think of him. Yes, I'll see you tomorrow at the meeting."

Flipping off the intercom, Kate opened and shut drawers in her desk, pretending to look for something. Betts came out and was surprised to find her still there.

"Kate, as long as you're here, I want you to do something for me. I smashed the crystal on my watch earlier. Could you take it to a jeweler and get a replacement for me? I know you have the day off tomorrow, but you can bring it to my house in the morning. Think you can do that? I just don't have the time."

"Certainly, Mr. Betts, I'd be more than happy to do that for you. I have to pick up something at the mall, so it'll be no trouble."

"I'll expect you around ten o'clock in the morning then. You have my home address, don't you?"

"Yes, I have it."

He handed over his watch and told her to be on her way.

Instead of the mall, she made a bee line home, and throwing her coat down on the chair, she all but ran to the phone. Hearing Reed's voice, she started in.

"Reed, can you come over right away, it's important," Kate hurried.

"I'm on my way," and the line went dead.

Kate fixed his drink and poured herself a glass of wine, put them in the den and waited for what she thought was an eternity. Finally, running to the door when she heard him knock, she flung it open and he rushed in. She led him to the den and they sat down on the couch.

"Reed, Betts called the president and told him you were snooping around, asking questions. I heard him tell Hastings that he knew you would be out of town till Monday; but Reed, he said that he's going to have you watched when you get back! How are you going to get anywhere with a tail on you?"

"Kat, calm down. Let's think this through. The last thing we need to do is panic. Evidently there's nothing to worry about till we get back from our holiday."

Reed picked up his drink, took a slow gulp and sat quietly in thought. Kate kept quiet to give him time to think and sat sipping her wine.

"I think we can get around that without a problem. First, we'll see if he does have me watched. If I need to, I'll book a flight out on Tuesday for New York City, so they think I'm leaving on assignment for the paper. I'll take the flight, make sure they aren't hanging around in New York, and then rent a car and drive back to D.C. I'll make sure it's known that I'll be gone till Thursday night when my show airs. When

I get back I should be home free. They're not going to keep a tail on an empty apartment. I'll just have to keep a low profile when I get back. If I'm spotted, then they'll know for sure something's up. Right now they just think I'm a pest that won't go away. There's no danger there, Kat, so please don't worry. If I hop an early morning flight, I can be back in town that night. It might be a good idea if I stayed here that night to make sure the tail is gone. Would that be acceptable to you?"

"Of course, Reed, you're more than welcome here. I'll feel better knowing that I'll have you under my watchful eye.

"Oh," she exclaimed, "speaking of watchful, I forgot all about the watch Betts gave me to get a crystal replaced for him. I'm supposed to get it fixed and drop it off at his home tomorrow morning at ten. I've got to run to the mall before it closes."

"You have Betts' watch? Kat, what a stroke of luck!"

Reed jumped up and dashed for the phone, dialing a number. "General, this is Reed. Kat has Betts' watch here to have it fixed for him. She's on her way to the mall for a new crystal. Is there any way we can get a bug placed in there before she returns it in the morning?"

"Go with her, Reed when she has it done, then the two of you come here. If I'm not back, wait. I'm on my way to pick up the bug. I know just the kind we'll need. I'll see you both here."

"You got it, General, we're on our way." Reed looked at Kate and smiled. "C'mon, Kat, we're off to bug a watch!"

The crystal replaced, they made their way to the Powers' house and arrived about eight forty-five. Knocking on the door, it immediately opened, and Helene let them in.

"Brad isn't back yet. He told me what's going on. I hope this works to our benefit. From what Brad has told me we need a breakthrough."

"I'm hoping for that too," Reed added. "If this is a watch that he wears all the time, we could very well pick up some pertinent information."

"It's the one he always wears, Reed; he's never without it. I'm sure that's why he's anxious for me to bring it by his house in the morning."

Just then Brad came rushing in with a couple of agents in tow.

"These are a couple of our guys, Reed. They're going to set up a receiving station here and one in a van that they'll have close to Betts wherever he goes. Give them the watch, Kate, and they'll fix it up nice and pretty," he grinned.

Kate handed over the watch, and while the two men busied themselves with their work, the four others conversed about possibilities.

A couple of hours later, the work and strategies all done and in place, Reed and Kate left with the watch. Reed went up to Kate's apartment with her, and came in for a hot cup of coffee. They sat down to relax and talk over the evening.

"I hope this works," Kate said.

"It can't hurt, Kat, and now, my sweet, let's put it aside and enjoy a few minutes before I have to leave."

He reached over and pulled Kate close and kissed her gently. They sat quietly in each other's arms and enjoyed the warmth. Soon Reed said he must go.

"It's after midnight, Kat, and you have a busy day ahead. I'll see you at the gala, and now, see me to the door, then get some rest."

They got up and made their way to the front door where Reed gave her a long, lingering kiss.

"Another job well done, love," he whispered.

"G'nite, Reed, and thank you for alleviating my fears."

"G'nite, Kat."

Chapter 8

Midmorning found Kate at the home of her boss. Caroline, Betts' wife, answered the door and asked her in. She summoned her husband who came out to the entry where Kate was waiting, chatting with Caroline.

"Did you have any trouble getting a new crystal?" he asked.

"None whatsoever, Mr. Betts," and handed the small box over to him.

"Jason would be lost without that watch. It's the one I gave him for our twentieth wedding anniversary. He tells me you'll be sitting at our table tonight, Kate."

"Yes, Mrs. Betts, and I'm looking forward to it. I hope to get the chance to finally meet the president and first lady in person."

"Well, Kate, I'm sure Jason will be happy to introduce you as we go through the reception line, won't you, Jason?"

"Uh, oh yes, yes," he said as he slipped on his watch and checked for the correct time.

"That would be kind of you, Mr. Betts, and thank you, Mrs. Betts, for your kindness. Now, I must be going."

"Please, call me Caroline. You needn't be so formal. We'll see you tonight then," she said as she opened the door for Kate.

"Yes, good-bye, Mr. Betts, good-bye.....Caroline."

Kate breathed a sigh of relief as she walked back to her car.

"Now we'll let the agents and the general take over," she mused as she got in and drove away.

The rest of the day was spent taking care of bills that had been neglected, straightening up the apartment and getting her clothes out that she planned to take on her trip home. She collected the packages that had to go with her and thought that she would have time to deliver the Powers' gifts to them before getting ready for the gala.

"I'll take Diane's also, since she wasn't at home earlier," Kate thought.

She would disburse the others when she got back from her grandparents. Grabbing her coat and packages, she started out.

Underneath the Pentagon, the five men gathered in their secret meeting room.

"I've called you here for the purpose of alleviating the fears that some of you have about Jessica's prying. You can all put it to rest. I assure you that it's been taken care of. There will be no more meddling from Jessica after tomorrow. And now, gentlemen, the path is clear to Rebirth!"

The clink of glasses and then Betts replied "Genesis, the Rebirth, may we all prosper in the new regime."

Back at the Powers' residence, Kate was ushered in with her gifts in tow. Helene took them from her, thanked her, and set them under the tree, then asked if she could get Kate something warm to drink. Kate declined saying that she had to rush back home to get ready for the big night. While they were talking, the general came in and told the two women what he had just heard.

"It sounds as if the president is going to ship Jessica off somewhere till this is over. I bet he had one hell of a fight when he issued that order."

The general then continued on to tell them the rest of what took place, about Genesis and the Rebirth, and their pompous toast.

Genesis—that's what I had found written on those notes in Betts' office. That must be their code name for their plot, and all the while I thought it was the name of a place. Genesis, which means the beginning, and Betts said Rebirth. They must be planning the Rebirth of our system of government. If they aren't stopped, we could witness the demise of our free republic. You were right, General, but we still don't know how they plan to accomplish their evil deeds. Do you and Reed still think it'll be done with terrorist-type bombs around the country?"

"Yes, Kate, we still go along with that theory, although I'm stumped by all the secrecy down at the Pentagon bunker. Now if you ladies will excuse me, I need to phone Reed and tell him what I've just told you."

"Of course General, I have to be on my way, so I'll say good-bye to you both. I'll look for you tonight."

"Wait, Kate," Helene said, as she went into another room and came back with a large prettily wrapped box.

"Thank you both for the present. G'bye for now."

They both wished her good-bye and Kate was off.

Back at home, she started to prepare for the gala, which was in just a couple of hours. She showered and washed her hair, then styled it in a becoming upsweep held in place with combs edged in gold. It took some time to accomplish this, as tiny wisps of hair kept falling loose. She finally decided to leave them. The wisps fell softly and actually added to the attractiveness of the whole look.

She donned a long satin cream skirt that had a side slit to above the knee, carefully slipped a plain cream satin shell over her head, added tiny diamond stud earrings and clasped a single diamond on a chain around her neck. She packed a couple of things in a gold evening bag and then put on a gold lame evening jacket to finish off her outfit. Slipping into her cream satin high heels, she gave a turn in front of the full-length mirror and decided she would pass muster with the elite she would be mingling with. She checked the clock and thought that she would just about make it on time if she left right away.

Making her way through the long entrance hall to the dining room, she waited to be escorted to her table. Mr. and Mrs. Hargraves, the Betts and Greg Hicks were already seated. Kate was introduced to Theresa Hargraves, who she had not met before and took her seat between Caroline Betts and Greg Hicks. Paul Robbins and his wife Edith came in shortly and took their seats to complete their table.

Kate marveled at the plush decorations. Their table sat directly in front of the fireplace that was lit with a gas flame. Above the mantle was a huge portrait of President Lincoln. The tables were covered with deep red cloths and the place settings were those purchased from France by President Monroe.

In the center of each table was a large bouquet of mixed red poppies and pink and white carnations, flanked by four very tall white tapers in gold candlesticks.

A Persian designed, soft green and brown carpet covered the floor. Kate gazed around in wonder, taking in the elegant room.

"Isn't it beautiful, Kate?" Caroline broke in.

"Oh, yes, and these place settings with their gilt edging are so delicate."

The two continued to converse for a few minutes, then Kate turned and spoke to Greg Hicks on subjects she thought would be of interest to him.

Before long, dinner was served, all five courses. When at last they rose to adjourn to the East Room where the reception line was forming, Kate was thankful for the chance to stretch and get some exercise.

They walked down the long hallway that led from one end of the

White House to the other, and emerged into the East Room. They all took their places in the receiving line and talked while they waited patiently to meet the Belkhanovs, the president and the first lady.

Kate's eyes wandered around the huge room and she spotted the general and Helene, but didn't see Reed. She stood admiring the Bohemian cut-glass chandeliers, and thought of how beautifully they had kept the room in its eighteenth century classical style. She glanced over at a full-length portrait of George Washington and couldn't help but wonder what he would have thought about the actions of this president.

Turning her attention back, she spoke to Caroline as they moved closer to their destination. It was finally Caroline's turn to shake hands with the first lady. Standing next to her were the Belkhanovs' and then the president.

Caroline moved on to greet the Russians and Betts stepped up to introduce Kate to Jessica. Jessica reached out and took Kate's hand. As their hands clasped, Kate experienced one of her visions.......she saw before her, a blinding flash of an airplane exploding in the air. She looked at the first lady and knew that she was doomed!

Trying to keep her composure, she said how glad she was to meet Jessica, and murmured something about this being a very special tribute to President Belkhanov and his wife Anna. Covering up her fear and barely keeping her wits about her, she wished the first lady a pleasant evening and moved on.

After issuing a warm greeting to Ivan and Anna Belkhanov, she stood facing the man she knew was planning to murder his own wife. Betts introduced them, and the president took her hand and noticed that she was trembling slightly.

"Take it easy, Kate, I won't bite. I'm pleased to finally get to meet the lovely voice on the phone, and one of our loyal, trusted employees."

"Thank you, Mr. President, I'm so pleased to finally have the privilege of meeting you personally."

"Kate, you continue your good work for Jason here, and you may just find yourself in a much better paid position before long, isn't that right, Jason?"

"Yes, yes, Kate does her job well, Mr. President. And now, Kate, we have to move along," Betts said.

They went to join Caroline and the Robbins. They all chatted until the reception line had concluded.

The entertainment followed with two well-known singing stars, performing two songs each, then the orchestra started the music for dancing.

Kate excused herself and went to the ladies room. She ran into Helene in there and the two emerged together. They found the general, and the three found a place to sit on a bench out of the way of all the hubbub.

"Have either of you seen Reed? I need to talk to the three of you tonight."

"He should be around somewhere, Kate," Helene said. "What's the matter, you look pale. Are you feeling all right?"

"I'm fine. I've just had a shock. I'll be okay in a few minutes. In fact, it would be a good idea if I mingled a bit."

Just then Reed appeared looking very handsome, indeed. Kate brightened at the sight of him. As had been prearranged, the general and Helene stood up to greet him, and they politely introduced him to Kate. That done, the general told Reed about Kate's wanting to meet with them later.

The music started up with a slow, romantic tune, and Reed very politely asked Kate to dance. Brad and Helene also moved onto the dance floor, as did many others. Reed could feel the tension in Kate as they glided to a waltz.

"What's the matter, Kat, my love," he whispered in her ear.

"I've had a rather shocking experience, Reed. I can't begin to explain it to you now. Will you, Helene and the general meet me at their house after this is over?"

"Of course, Kat. I'll tell them and we'll see you there. Meantime, I don't think we should see each other the rest of the evening. We don't want to create any suspicion."

"You're right, of course, and I'll excuse myself and seek out some of the others."

They finished their dance, and Kate moved on across the room to where Betts and his wife were in conversation with the Hargraves.

"Hello Kate, are you enjoying yourself?" Caroline queried.

"Yes, very much. What a delightful, elegant affair."

"I saw you dancing with Reed Adams, Kate. I wasn't aware that you knew him," Jason inquired with veiled eyes.

"I was just introduced to him, and he was kind enough to ask me to dance."

"He's a bad one, Kate, I'd stay away from him if I were you. He's nothing but trouble where the White House is concerned," Betts warned. "Was he asking you any questions?"

"No, Mr. Betts, he was very polite, and we didn't talk much while we danced."

Satisfied, Betts let it drop and went on conversing with John

Hargraves. Kate visited with the women for a time, then excused herself to go over to others she knew from the White House.

The gala was winding down, and Kate decided the time was right for her to make her exit. She sought out the Betts and thanked them for their kindness, said good night to the others and left through the north entrance.

She decided to make a stop at the apartment to change clothes before going on to the meeting.

About a half hour later she pulled up in front of the Powers' residence and saw the others were already there, so she hurried up the walk and rang the doorbell. Helene asked her in and offered her some coffee or a drink.

"I'll have some coffee please, Helene."

They all sat down in the living room and Kate began talking.

"I should begin by telling you that I have this gift. I can see things that are about to happen. I know it sounds weird, but it's true. I foresaw the death of my parents in a terrible automobile accident, and on another occasion saw the recent earthquake in California. I won't go into detail about it, it's what is called being a Sensitive. Tonight, when I shook hands with the first lady, I experienced a vision—a horrible fiery explosion of a plane in the air. I fear the president is behind it. Remember what he said at the meeting about not having to worry about Jessica after Friday?"

"Kat, are you saying that you actually saw this?"

"Yes, Reed, it was vivid. "There was no mistaking what it meant."

"If you're right, Kate, we'll have to try to stop it, but I don't know how we'd gain access to the airplane she's going to fly on," the general put in.

"I've read some about this gift you possess, and I certainly believe you," Helene offered. "There have been many times when the Government called in Sensitives to help in some complex cases. We need to take what Kate says very seriously," she stated, looking at the others.

"I'll see what I can do to find out what aircraft she'll be flying on and try our best to get it checked out," the general said.

He excused himself and went to make a phone call. He returned in about ten minutes and related his intentions to the group.

"I just ordered two experts in explosives to try to gain access to the first lady's plane and give it a thorough going over. That is if they can. You two are leaving tomorrow for the holiday, isn't that right?"

"Yes, General, Kat and I leave late tomorrow morning."

"Okay, well, let's just hope we're able to stop this. Now, you two get on home and have a great Christmas. Whatever happens, we'll do what we can."

Reed and Kate wished the general good luck, and said Merry Christmas to them both, and got up to leave. They walked together, hand in hand to their cars and kissed good night.

"I'll see you on the plane tomorrow, my love."

"Till then," Kate responded as they parted and went their separate ways.

Chapter 9

The morning was gray and overcast, but Kate's spirits were bright and sunny. The thought of spending the holiday in the country with Reed made her tingle with pleasure. She breezed through her breakfast, took a soothing shower and started dressing and preparing for the trip north.

She made it to the airport an hour early, got her luggage checked in, and found her way to the gate. She took a seat and opened the newspaper she brought from home to the crossword puzzle. Shortly before boarding time, she glanced up and spotted Reed, but continued on with the puzzle, paying him no attention.

Soon they called her flight number and she rose to get in line. Aboard the plane, she located her seat, put her things in the overhead and sat down to patiently wait for the rest of the passengers to board.

She saw Reed enter, making his way down the aisle toward her, and noting that the seat next to Kate was occupied, politely asked the woman if she would mind exchanging seats with him. The lady nicely agreed and moved her things three rows back.

"That's better. We have to savor all the time together that we can," he said with a grin.

The plane took off and climbed swiftly to leveling off altitude and the two settled back for the ride. They expressed hopes that the explosives experts were able to gain access to the first lady's plane and abort the calamity that awaited her.

Reed told Kate that there was nothing they could do about the first lady's plight, so suggested that they turn their attention to more pleasant topics.

"How about you telling me about Elmira and the area. I could use a bit of a history lesson, if you're in the mood."

"I'd be delighted to," Kate smiled, as she started telling him about the countryside around her grandparents' home.

"Elmira was originally named Newtown, where General Sullivan fought a decisive Revolutionary War battle. He was under orders from Washington to wipe out the Tories and Indians, which he did, then he moved on to destroy the Senecas' villages. They never recovered from that siege, and it heralded the end to the great Iroquois Nation. Later, renamed Elmira, it was a booming industrial city at the turn of this century. Mark Twain is a big part of their history, did you know that?"

"No," said Reed, "I've always heard his name connected with Hannibal, Missouri."

"Well," Kate continued, "he and his family are buried in Elmira. He married an Elmira girl, Olivia Langdon, and they spent many summers visiting with relatives there. His sister-in-law resided on a hill just outside of town, overlooking the Chemung River and the valley below. They called their home Quarry Farm, and she even had a study built for him out on the lawn, where he spent a good deal of time writing some of his most popular works. The study has since been moved into town and sets on the campus of Elmira College.

"Ever since the flood of nineteen seventy-two, which devastated the downtown area, the city has been struggling to bring it back to life, she added sadly. I only wish the leaders there could realize what a quaint town it used to be and try to revive it in that mode, instead of trying to bring a nineties look to it, which really doesn't enhance the beauty of its era."

"I think I know what you're saying, Kat. It's the quaintness and history of a place that gives it appeal," Reed said.

"But," replied Kate, "there really is no comparison to the beautiful countryside there. I sometimes think of the Iroquois and how lucky they were to live in and around that area."

As Kate sat in silent reverie, the pilot announced their descent into the regional airport. Soon they were gliding down the runway to a stop. Gathering their things, they made their way into the little terminal.

Pat was there to greet them.

"Gramps! It's so good to see you."

After giving him a big hug, she turned to Reed and introduced the two men.

"Kate didn't tell us that you were "the" Reed Adams," Pat grinned. "We see your television show most every week."

"Well, thank you, Mr. Malloy, I'm happy to hear that someone is out there in my television audience."

"Please, Reed, call me Pat. Mr. Malloy sounds very formal, and we are anything but that around here."

"All right, Pat it is."

They went to claim their luggage, then piled into Pat's car for the ride home.

"These rolling hills certainly hold a lot of charm," Reed remarked, as they meandered through the back roads. "Kat, I can see why you love the countryside here. I'm sure it must be something to behold in the spring and fall."

"Oh, it is," she exclaimed. "But I even find it beautiful when the ground is covered with snow, like today. Gramps, have you heard any late reports on the predicted snow for tonight?"

"Yep, sure have, and they say that a pretty good storm is moving our way. It should reach us by late evening, so it looks as though we're gonna have us a very white Christmas!"

Reed spoke up.

"I notice, Pat, that we haven't reached town yet. How far is the airport from the city?"

Pat laughed. "It's not far at all, Reed. I'm just taking the back roads cause I know Kate enjoys them more than the city streets."

So Reed settled in and remarked on different points of interest to him as they hummed along at a leisurely pace.

"I didn't tell you, Reed, but Elmira has always been known as the soaring capital of the country. Many, many years there were glider pilots that came from all over the world to compete, and Gram and Gramps used to take me up to Harris Hill to watch them take off over the valley. You could hear the swooshing of the gliders in the air, but it was so quiet without any motors. They used to remind me of hawks circling around in the air, silent and graceful."

"I've never had the pleasure of watching gliders on the wing, but I can imagine it's a peaceful, calming event to watch," Reed surmised.

Kate kept up the chatter with both her Gramps and Reed for the rest of the pleasurable ride home.

Before long, Pat pulled the car into the driveway at the side of their home. Reed remarked on the beauty of the one hundred fifty-year-old Greek Revival home.

"I see the outdoor lights are ready to turn on tonight, Gramps, and the candles are set in all the windows, too. The soft candle glow always looks so warm and inviting. Did you and Gram put the tree up yet?" Kate asked as they unloaded the car and made their way through the back door.

"I cut a big one earlier today and have it set up. Gram and I put the lights on, but she thought maybe you two kids would enjoy doin' the trimming."

Maggie came running into the kitchen and threw her arms around Kate and gave her a big kiss. Turning to Reed, she grinned, having recognized him.

"Well, Reed Adams, my word. Kate, for heaven's sake child, why didn't you tell us we would be entertaining a celebrity."

Kate laughed. "He's anything but a celebrity this weekend, Gram."

"Kat's right, Mrs. Malloy, I'm here as just a guy that thinks the world of your granddaughter," he smiled.

"Maggie will do just fine, Reed."

"All right, Maggie."

Maggie showed Reed to his room, while Kate took her things into her old room.

Rejoining them, Kate said "Reed, if you like, we can unpack and then I'll take you on a tour so you can familiarize yourself with the place."

"I'd like that, Kat. Come and get me when you have your things put away."

She ushered Reed around the house, then asked him to follow her up the short flight of stairs that led to the third floor walk-in attic.

"This is my favorite room," she said sighing. "I used to come up here and spend hours digging around among all Gram and Gramps' old things. This is my most favorite thing of all," she told him, as she opened a big old worn trunk. She lifted out several different costumes that were in very small sizes.

"These are Halloween costumes that Gram made for me to wear trick-or-treating. My mom couldn't sew at all, so that chore fell to Gram. This Flamenco dancer was a favorite, and so was this little Dutch girl, but I think the one I had the most fun in was this clown."

Putting the costumes neatly away, she glanced up at Reed. Catching him in a far away look, she urged him to reveal his thoughts.

"I was thinking back to all the fun that we had as children when everything was so simple. For instance, we could only trick-or-treat at houses of those people that we knew, and we would have to stand there while they guessed who we were. Then when they unmasked us, they would give us each an apple, or a piece of penny candy, or if we were real lucky, we might receive a penny! That was the fun of Halloween, to see how long it took them to figure out who we were, and it made us quite creative in finding just the right get-ups to wear."

"We did have good times when we were young, didn't we," Kate interjected. "Now, people are afraid to send their children out, for fear of something being put into their goodies, and it has become so very commercialized. The children of today have no idea how to enjoy the true traditions of our holidays. It's very sad."

Putting the tray back on top of the costumes, she lifted out two little porcelain bride and groom Kewpies.

"These cuties were on the top of my grandparents' wedding cake," she said, carefully showing them to Reed.

"I can well imagine you up here looking over these treasures and wistfully dreaming of the past. There looks to be a lifetime of memories within these walls," he said soothingly.

"It is a wonderful getaway for me and always has been through the years—a calming place to lose myself for a time," she smiled. "But for now, we'd best get ourselves downstairs for Gram's Christmas Eve dinner, or she'll be coming to look for us," she grinned.

Maggie had dinner laid out on the dining room table, looking very enticing to say the least, for they hadn't eaten since the light lunch on the plane. They all sat down, Pat said the blessing and started passing the sumptuous platters of food around the table. They all chattered merrily away, catching up on each other's doings. After they finished their dessert of warm bread pudding, the men got up and excused themselves. They offered their help, but the ladies shooed them away, and Maggie told them to go turn on the television and catch the latest news.

The ringing of the phone stopped Pat on his way to the living room. He lifted the receiver and said a cheery hello.

"It's for you, Reed," and handed the phone over.

He continued on into the living room, so Reed could carry on a private conversation.

"Hello, Reed, this is Brad. I'm sorry to bother you, but you need to know what happened. Have you seen any news reports?"

"We were just about to turn on the news. I take it you're calling to say that the men weren't successful in stopping the tragedy?"

"Well, it's all over the news as you'll soon see. Kate was right. The first lady's plane exploded in midair. Blew the plane to pieces! We tried what we could, but security was tighter than I've ever seen it; there was just no way we could get our guys in. It looks like our dear president has just done in his wife! I'll let you go, I just wanted you and Kate to know that we did our best. There's nothing to be done, so I want you two to enjoy yourselves, and we'll talk when you return to D.C. By the way Reed, they're putting it out that it was a terrorist bomb and blaming Murabi."

"Okay, General, I'll relay your news to Kat. You and Helene have a good Christmas."

"You too, Reed. Good-bye."

Reed joined Pat in the living room and saw that he was listening to the report of the first lady's disastrous end. After the ladies finished in the kitchen, they joined the men to watch some of the coverage.

Maggie, noting the downcast looks on the young ones, suggested that they get started on the tree trimming to try to get their minds off the tragedy.

She had already hung garlands from the mantle and down the open staircase, giving the house a warm, festive look.

Pat had a fire glowing in the den fireplace, and since it had grown dark, he turned on the outside lights. Maggie went around and switched on all the candles in the windows and informed everyone that it had started to snow.

"You children are going to midnight Mass with us, aren't you?"

"Yes, Gram, it's such a lovely service. We'll get ready as soon as we're finished with the tree."

Reed remarked that he didn't know how Pat had gotten such a mammoth tree in the house by himself. Kate laughed and told him that Gramps did it every year.

The next two hours were spent joking and enjoying each other. Reed had told Kate about the general's phone call and then said the rest of their time here was to be spent worry free.

"No more talk of Washington, Kat. We're here for a festive holiday and that's exactly what we're going to enjoy."

"You don't have to tell me twice, Reed. Let's begin right now."

Maggie came in and asked if they were ready for a drink or hot chocolate. They both opted for the latter, and soon Maggie returned with a tray and set it on the coffee table. She had baked some Christmas cookies and fruit breads and had a plate full for them to choose from.

"Spending Christmas Eve this way, Kat, sure brings back warm thoughts of my younger years and Christmas at home. In our family, we also decorated the tree on Christmas Eve. Each one of us had our part to do. We had some of the funniest looking Christmas trees anyone ever laid eyes on," he laughed. "Then on Christmas morning, no one was allowed downstairs until we were all gathered together. My mom would make us line up by age, starting with the youngest, till we looked like our own stair steps. Then we would march in a line down to the den where the tree was laden with presents. We would get to open one present, and then we had to eat before opening all the rest. My dad would play Santa, and would give each gift to the youngest, who got to deliver them to the rest of the family. Only one person at a time could open their present, so that we all could see what everyone got. You can imagine, Kat, that it took hours for us to finish, what with nine in the family."

"Reed, I think that sounds like a lovely tradition, and I'm sure that it was a good lesson in teaching all of you children patience," she grinned.

They continued on with their gigantic task, teasing one another and laughing at each other's antics. Finally, hand-in-hand ,they stepped back to survey their handiwork. Satisfied, Reed reached down and clicked on the lights.

"It's so beautiful," Kate cooed.

"It is that," Reed remarked, slipping his arms around her waist.

He reached down and kissed her neck, sending quivers up and down her body. She leaned back against him and enjoyed the warmth of him. They stood that way for several minutes, when at last Kate moved and turned to face him. She raised her head up and gave him a long tender kiss.

Maggie and Pat walked in and took in the scene before them, looked at each other and grinned, then Maggie broke in.

"We'd better get ready for church. We don't have far to go, but with the snow it'll take longer to get there."

Kate and Reed made a beeline for their rooms, changed clothes and were ready to go in fifteen minutes. Meanwhile, Pat had cleaned up the den of boxes and soon they were on their way.

"Mass is at St. Mary's," Kate told Reed. "It's the church where I was baptized. I also attended grammar school there."

"Aha, so it's the good nuns of St. Mary's that molded my Kat," he smiled.

They soon entered the old church and enjoyed a beautiful candlelight service with the choir singing the hymns of Christmas. After the service, Kate met a few old friends, introduced Reed to them and wished them all a merry Christmas.

Reaching home, they set to the task of piling all the gifts under the tree. Pretty tired from their busy day, they all wished each other a good night and retired for a well deserved sleep.

Christmas morning proved to be a winter wonderland. Pat and Maggie had risen early, turned on all the Christmas lights and while Pat started a roaring fire in the fireplace, Maggie set out to prepare her special Christmas breakfast.

By the time Kate and Reed descended the stairs, the sweet aroma of fresh baked cinnamon rolls blended with the smell of bacon and fresh-brewed coffee.

They stopped to look out the window and Kate oohed at the beautiful sight.

"It looks like a Currier and Ives picture out there this morning, Reed. Look out toward the pond and the woods—have you ever seen anything to compare?"

"It is something to behold," he murmured, taking in the scene.

Moving on, ambling out to the kitchen, Maggie motioned for them to sit down while she poured their coffee. Soon the four were having an enjoyable breakfast, and discussing the beautiful country scene out the window.

Maggie shooed them off to the den when they finished eating and said she would bring in more coffee. Kate and Reed plopped down on the sofa in front of the fire while Pat distributed the gifts.

Kate noticed a tiny box that was from Reed. She decided to leave it till last. One by one they opened their gifts. Reed opened his from Kate and beamed with pleasure.

"I'll cut the tags off and put it on for our walk that you promised me today, Kat," he grinned.

Kate sat with the last little box in her lap and began to unwrap it. Lifting the cover she brought out a beautiful pin. It was a gold cat with two emerald eyes.

"Oh, Reed, it's gorgeous! Thank you so much!"

"I thought it a perfect gift for my green-eyed Kat," he said softly, smiling.

She reached over and kissed him soundly.

Kate and Maggie proceeded to clean up the mess of wrapping paper and ribbons, then went to the kitchen to clean up the breakfast dishes. Pat and Reed spent the time getting to know one another better.

Finished with all the clean-up, Kate came in and announced that she was ready for their outside adventure, so they bundled up, with Reed donning his new sweater.

It was still snowing lightly and the two started off down the lane that led past the pond to the woods.

"This is beautiful country, Kat. It gives one an inner peace to look around at the serenity. It's not hard to forget that the world is in chaos."

Kate nodded, then pulled him out onto the frozen pond where they slipped and slid around till their sides ached from laughing. Then for the next couple of hours, they plodded through the snow, stopping now and then to throw snow balls at one another, or just to rest and look up at the falling white flakes.

Working their way back to the house, Kate plopped herself down in the snow and proceeded to lay on her back, moving her arms up and down to make a snow angel. She got up laughing and Reed took her in his arms. Planting a long hard kiss on her lips, he moved his head back slightly, looked into her laughing eyes and said in a hoarse whisper

"Kat, my green-eyed Kat, how I love you."

"I love you, Reed. I've loved you from the first moment we met."

"Kat, when all this mess is over with, and it will be soon, one way or another, will you marry me?"

Kate put her hand up to his face and caressed it.

"Yes, oh yes, Reed. To be your wife would fulfill my greatest wish. Nothing in this world would mean anything if I didn't have you in it, sharing everything with me. To sleep in your arms each night and wake up seeing your smiling face each morning. To have your children," then she hesitated. "You do want children, don't you?"

"As many as you think we can handle," he laughed. "Kat, my love, You've made me deliriously happy," and he picked her up in his arms and twirled her around until they both fell into the snow laughing.

Finally reaching the house, they kicked off their snow-covered boots and coats, and went looking for Maggie and Pat. When they told them their news, hugs, kisses and handshakes made the rounds.

"Reed," Kate said, "I hope I'll have a chance to meet all your family before we marry. What do you suppose they'll think of this?"

"Sweet Kat, my family will think you're the best thing that has ever come into my life. Trust me, they're all going to be delighted. And yes, I'll make sure you meet them all, the whole bloomin' bunch," he laughed.

And so on went the day, with friends stopping by with trays of homemade goodies, and happy conversations. Christmas night found the women chatting quietly while the men challenged each other to chess. After a most pleasant day they all turned in early.

All too soon it was time to pack up and leave for the airport. Maggie rode along with them and chattered away at how happy she was for the both of them and that Kate had better let them know about their future plans. Kate, promising she would, said she may even want a formal wedding, but they would have to talk that over when the time came.

Pulling into the parking lot, Pat and Reed saw to the luggage, and they checked in. The call to board the plane came over the speaker, and good-byes were hurriedly given, and soon the two were in the air.

"Kat, I can't remember a more enjoyable time, and it's all because of you."

"I've loved every minute of it, Reed. I hate to have it end."

"When we land, we get off separately and go our own way," Reed told her. "I'm not going to contact you until I drive back from New York City. I'll come directly to your apartment. Are we in agreement on that?"

"Yes, of course, Reed, you can't take any chances. We certainly know that they're eliminating anyone who gets in their way. I'll be trying to find out more, if possible. I don't know if I'll have to work tomorrow due to the plane tragedy. I'll have to check."

So with their plans understood, they enjoyed the rest of the time they had together. Reed put his arm around Kate and pulled her close, nuzzling her hair and whispering words of love in her ear. She thought she had never felt so happy, and snuggled in closer.

Chapter 10

Kate was up and moving in the early morning hours, having found a message on her answering machine from Betts when she arrived home from her holiday. It was there along with a message from Bill wishing her a merry Christmas.

The airwaves were humming with news of the first lady's demise, and that all available efforts were being made to apprehend the terrorist who planted the bomb aboard her plane.

The White House was reporting about the upcoming funeral service and the dignitaries who would attend.

Also in the news were reports of new spreading ethnic confrontations in Rwanda. It was getting severe enough that President Hastings had issued a warning that if the bloodshed didn't come to a halt, he would send in several thousand ground troops to quell the atrocities there. His mission was to force peace on all the warring factions, or the United States would step in. This would mean that he would move some troops that were already in Macedonia to Rwanda, and ship five thousand more from the States.

"That will leave next to none here at home," Kate told herself. "What is his purpose in invading these countries.? These confrontations have been going on for hundreds of years in all of these countries, and it's just now that the president sees fit to try to stop the slaughter. He's got to know that no one, either here or abroad, goes along with this aggression," she mused.

Hearing enough, she turned off the radio, picked up her coat and purse and headed out to work. The message left by Betts asked her to come in, so she would see what was on his agenda today.

D.C. was quiet on the early morning drive to the White House. There was barely a car on the roads.

"It's as if the town had died over the holiday," she thought.

Snow was piled up at the curbs, leaving everything dirty, cold and depressing. Congress had adjourned until after the New Year, and most of the press had already moved out to cover the memorial service in Tennessee for the first lady.

Making her way into her office, she found Betts already busy at his desk. When he saw her enter, he came out with a bunch of papers in his hand.

"Good morning, Mr. Betts. It's such a tragedy about the first lady. I know you are a close friend of both the president and his wife and I'm sorry for your loss," she put in.

"Yes, yes, a tragic loss to be sure. The president is in deep mourning," he said rather contritely. "Now, Kate, I'll be leaving this afternoon for the memorial service and will be gone until Wednesday. I'll stay over Tuesday night and fly back with the president late the next morning. Right now I need you to type up these statements for me. They have to be ready by one o'clock. Do you think you can manage it?"

"Of course, sir, I'll have them ready for you."

"I want you to come to work even though I'll be gone. I have quite a few documents that I need you to type up and have ready for me by New Year's Eve. I thought I'd have plenty of time, but with this unexpected tragedy, it's going to tighten my schedule. These are to be kept strictly secret, Kate, there can be no word of these getting out, at least not until next week. You are privy to previewing some very important changes coming shortly after the New Year. Do you understand what I'm saying to you, Kate? If this is made known there will be dire consequences," he finished.

"I understand, Mr. Betts," she replied rather tersely.

"All right then, I'll leave you to your work," and back into his office he strode.

As she typed away, she took a few phone calls, putting them through to Betts. She knew she needn't bother listening in, since they were still monitoring him by means of the bug.

She didn't have any visitors as most offices were closed down. Once in a while, she noticed a shadow passing by her office door, but that was the extent of it. She worked straight through and finished the work by twelve thirty.

The statements were to inform the people that every measure was being taken to prevent other such bombings. Every airport in the country had put double security on passengers and on the planes themselves. The federal agents and the FBI were on the lookout for any clue to the whereabouts of one Jabar Murabi, the known terrorist.

"The president is certainly playing this to the hilt," Kate thought. "They don't seem to care how much trouble they're causing the airlines with their phony baloney story. Whatever it takes to cover their own criminal hides. Nothing like keeping all the Federal Agents busy on a wild goose chase, and they've even got the general public scared to death to go anywhere, for fear of random bombs going off anyplace or anywhere. What a sham!"

Betts came in at one and she had the material ready and in a folder for him.

"Take the rest of the day off, Kate, and get a fresh start on those documents tomorrow. When you go home each day, put them in the top drawer of my desk and lock it. I don't want prying eyes to see them."

"Yes, Mr. Betts."

"Well, I'm off to the biggest media circus of the year. Those idiots thrive on wars and tragedies. Heh, heh, they'll no doubt be in their glory next week," he hissed so low it was barely discernible, and with a curt wave of his hand, he was gone.

"He reminds me of a slithering snake," Kate mumbled to herself.

Reed was spending his day writing his column and setting up his guests for his Thursday program.

He had already taken note of the strange car parked across the street and down a-ways. He figured Betts kept his word about putting a tail on him.

"Well," he thought, "this guy's going to get mighty bored with his duty today."

He put in a phone call to make his airplane reservations to New York City the next morning and then made a leisurely drive to the airport to pick up his ticket. He wanted to make sure his tail knew exactly where he was headed. He went up to the reservation counter and received his ticket, then headed back toward the exit. Before he went out the door he made sure his guy was getting the information on his flight and satisfied, meandered back to his car for the drive home.

He got down a suitcase and filled it, adding extra clothes that he would need at Kate's. He placed a call to the general and told him of his plans and asked if he had anything else of interest.

"We've been monitoring Betts constantly, and we got what he said to Kate earlier. Seems she has some secret documents to get ready for him. Something, he said, that will be used next week." The general went on. "I'm sure Kate will let you know what they're about when you see her tomorrow night. One of my agents reports that the "big five" have another meeting planned for Friday night at eleven o'clock.

Oh, and Reed, they've changed the coding at the Missile Launch Center. I was going to slip in today and my card is no good. It's locked up tight. When I questioned the guard, he said it was ordered changed by the president, because of the terrorist bombing of the first lady's plane. I'm wondering if they're planning to use a missile or two if they have any trouble putting their martial law into effect. The threat of a nuclear bomb would certainly squelch any attempt at rebellion."

"I don't know what to make of that, General. We've got four days to try and find out exactly what they do have planned. They're pushing this terrorist thing to the max, using the first lady's disaster to promote their plan. We've got to find out where they've placed these so-called terrorist bombs around the country, if indeed that's the plan, and as of now, we don't have anything else to go on. Once those bombs go off we're lost, General. We won't have a prayer of proving the president responsible."

"You're right, of course, Reed, no one would believe him capable of such an act. One other thing, I have the blueprints of the Pentagon and have been going over them. If you can get with me Wednesday, I want to talk over a possibility with you."

"I'll make it a point to get out to your place, General, however, I want to make sure I'm not followed."

Their business over, they ended their conversation. Reed got back to work putting the finishing touches on his column and made some phone calls, setting up his panel of guests for his Thursday talk show. He had lined up a group to discuss the possible glitches from Y2K. That taken care of, he headed out the door to his favorite restaurant for a late dinner.

Kate had just finished dinner and was waiting for Bill to arrive. He had phoned earlier and asked to come over. When she heard him at the door, she went and escorted him to the den. She had wanted to see him for her own reasons.

Bill handed her a gift that he had for her and she opened it to find a book that he knew she was wanting to read. She thanked him for remembering, and then went to her little tree and returned with a gift she had for him. He opened it and grinned when he saw it was a model kit for the F-117 Stealth Fighter. His hobby was building model airplanes and he had a large collection that went back to a model of the Wright Brothers' first airborne craft.

"Thanks, Kate, this will be a great addition to my gallery of planes."

Kate took the wrappings and ribbons out to the trash and returned to join him.

"How was your trip home, Kate? Did you have a good visit with your grandparents?"

"Sure did, Bill. It was difficult to leave, not really wanting to come back with all the bad news about the first lady."

"There's no sense beating around the bush, Kate, so I'm just going to come out with it. I ran into my old girlfriend over the holiday. She's just gotten divorced, and we've kinda struck an understanding, and we're going to see if we can make a go of it this time. I'm hoping that we can remain friends, Kate, but I'm going to have to cancel on our dates," he finished.

"Oh Bill, I'm so happy for you. I've had a feeling that you still had a thing for Mary Jo, the way you would bring her name up in our conversations. It is Mary Jo, isn't it?"

"Was I so obvious, Kate?" he said blushing.

Kate was so relieved that she didn't have to be the one to call it quits with Bill, that she was fairly bubbling over.

"It's all right, I'm truly glad for you. And of course we'll remain friends. That's all we've ever been really, and there certainly are no bad feelings from this end."

"Thanks, Kate, and now I'd better get going. I told Mary Jo that I was going to see you tonight to explain, and she wants me to phone her and tell her how it went."

Kate laughed. "Well, you tell her that I couldn't be happier for the both of you."

She got up and walked Bill to the door, and they wished each other luck and said good-bye.

"Talk about good timing," she said to herself. "I couldn't have planned that any better if I tried."

Feeling like a load had been lifted off her shoulders, Kate made her way to the shower. Afterward, she slipped on her robe and settled down to watch the television coverage of the first lady.

From the news reports that she had heard earlier, quite a few dignitaries were traveling in to Bluff City, Tennessee for the memorial service, and to pay their respects. Bluff City was Jessica's home town, and the service was going to be held at the Methodist Church there.

She pulled her feet up under her and started to flip channels. All the big three networks were carrying something on the tragedy. One was in Bluff City covering the arrival of dignitaries, and other happenings in and around the town.

Another was doing interviews from a small cafe in town, getting the reactions of the hometown folk.

The other station had opted to do a syrupy, overblown special on Jessica's life, and contributions she made to the betterment of the country she loved so much. The way the narrator spoke of her, she was only one step below sainthood.

Kate watched bits and pieces of the different shows for a little over an hour, then decided to call it a night. She climbed into bed, and turned her thoughts to tomorrow night when she would see Reed. Soon she was fast asleep.

Chapter 11

The airplane took off with Reed aboard heading for New York City. He had seen his bodyguard, the tail, standing at the gate as he looked out from his window seat.

“Good,” he thought, “he didn’t board with me. Now we’ll see if he has a friend at the other end.”

He sat back and mentally went over his plans for the day. It was a short flight, and he came into JFK International terminal, claimed his luggage and headed out the door.

Alert to everyone around him he kept a close eye out for anybody looking suspicious. Hailing a cab, he climbed in and gave the cabby the address of his newspaper. As they pulled out and into traffic, Reed kept a sharp eye out for any car following the same route.

One car followed for a time, then sped up to pass. Reed noticed a young couple in the car as they passed by.

“Okay, he told himself, it looks like I’m home free. Obviously they don’t find me that much of a threat. As long as I’m out of town and out of their hair, I’m of no importance.”

Pulling up in front of his home office, Reed got out and gave the cabby a large tip and proceeded into the building. He knocked on his editor’s door and was asked to come in. Handing over his column he told Jake that as long as he was in town on business he thought he’d hand deliver it. The editor, Jake Fairbanks, was glad to see him and asked if he had time to have lunch with him. Reed accepted and the two set out for Mama Leone’s, a favorite of Jake’s.

The two men ate a leisurely lunch and talked business. Jake had some ideas for Reed to use in his upcoming columns and they hashed over the possibilities. His editor was well aware that Reed did his own thing and made it clear that he was only handing out suggestions.

They finished lunch and headed back to the office. All the while Reed kept a close watch for any signs of a tail. He was confident he was not being followed here in the City.

Back at the office, Reed asked to use the phone and called for a rental car. Saying good-bye to Jake, he made his way to the street below and hailed a cab. In no time they arrived at the car rental agency, and Reed paid the driver, took his luggage in hand and headed into the building. Soon he was settled in a late model sedan and calmly started his trek back to D.C.

About fifty miles down the thruway, he thought that he may have been wrong about not having a tail. Having noticed that this same car had stayed behind him from the time he got on the thruway, he figured he had better find out for sure. He spotted a turnoff ahead, and veered off, down the ramp and into the parking lot of a diner.

Getting out and entering the eatery, he saw that indeed the trailing car was pulling into the parking lot. He went on to a booth where he would be able to see if he was followed inside and by whom.

The waitress brought him the coffee and sweet roll that he ordered, and he ate slowly. Finally getting up and paying his tab, he sauntered back to his car and started out for the interstate on-ramp.

Moving up behind him was the same tan car. Instead of getting on the interstate, he took a right and started down the access road. The tail, knowing that he had been spotted, decided to end this little game. He sped up and came along side Reed's car, and tried to force him off the road.

"Guess they think I'm more of a pest than I thought. Don't know how I missed this guy, he must have picked up my trail going to the rental," Reed muttered, trying to keep the car steadied.

The car came up on him once again, and Reed floored it and took off, but to no avail. This went on for what seemed to Reed an eternity; both vehicles swerving in and out of traffic, and narrowly missing cars as they sped by.

Reed saw a long empty stretch ahead. His pursuer along side tried to ram into him. He slammed on his brakes as the other car zoomed out in front. Before the other car could slow down, Reed floored the gas pedal again, pulled up along side, and quickly swerved. His car rammed into the side of the other, sending the tan car off the road flipping end over end until finally it burst into flames.

Reed had a time keeping his own car in an upright position, but got it under control and braked to a stop. Taking time to get his nerves under control, he then backed up to where the other car was in flames. Reed figured that the guy was dead, and when he heard sirens in the distance, he thought that he'd better make himself scarce. He stepped on the gas and took the first on ramp he saw and was soon back on the interstate.

"God, I hope I don't have the state police on my tail. That's all I need to bring attention to what's going on."

He started to feel his confidence return about a hundred miles down the road and decided to stop for a cup of coffee, which he did, and then was back for the last leg of his trip home.

Kate, far from calm, was trying to get through her day at work. She was there to prepare the procedural documents as instructed by her boss. When she scanned through them, she couldn't believe her eyes. They were road maps to a complete and total takeover by the president.

The first one outlined the president's plan of action upon declaring martial law. His first order of business would be to disband Congress and set aside the Constitution. This was an automatic procedure taken by any president that would have to declare martial law.

"Only it's supposed to be a temporary situation," Kate thought, "not a permanent one, which Hastings has in mind."

Then it went on to say that he would declare himself to be the sole enforcer of law in the country. She went on to read about the raising of the federal income tax, property and school taxes, and the federal takeover of all media, telecommunications, computer networks, medical, power companies, education and a drastic increase in sales taxes on all consumer items.

The second folder outlined the movements of the president's "Home Army," their directives for keeping order in the cities and towns, and what to do in case of uprisings or riots, and what measures were to be taken if this happens.

The next one held instructions and orders on the confiscation of weapons. The commanders of the new army, who were already in place in every city across the country, had computer printouts of every registered gun owner in their areas. Their instructions were to conduct a door-to-door confiscation. If they ran across anyone who refused to relinquish their arms, they were to take whatever means necessary to make them comply.

Another folder held orders and instructions for ousting the state, county and city officials. Once they were out, there would be one federal appointed head of each state that would report and take orders directly from the president.

The last folder stated the procedures for issuing national identification numbers to every man, woman and child in the country. These ID cards would have to be shown by anyone traveling from state to state or out of the country. They would also be used for banking procedures and just for purchasing goods.

Kate sat there at her desk stunned, feeling like she was sitting smack dab in the middle of the Twilight Zone.

"Good Lord," she whispered, "I'm reading about the complete and total downfall of our country; the end of our republic, our Constitution, and our freedoms. This president is a diabolical maniac, and from the looks of these documents, he has everything in place to make this happen."

Shaking herself out of her stupor, she willed herself to get started. It would take her a couple of days to get through all of this and she had to have it done by Friday. With shaky fingers, she began to type.

Off in a small town in Tennessee a solemn service was in progress for the first lady, Jessica Rusby Hastings. The little church was packed and overflow crowds lined the streets outside. Media cameras were everywhere and so was the Secret Service.

The commentators spoke in low, respectful tones, describing the scene and pointing out the dignitaries.

Throughout the entire service the cameras focused mainly on the president who sat alone in the front pew. His face serious and sad, he listened to the eulogies paying homage to his beloved wife. Every now and then his hand would reach up and brush a heartfelt tear from his eye. The public was witnessing a sorrowful, devastated president.

When the service ended, a solemn, head-bent low president, made his way out of the church.

The others followed after the president went through the doors. There was an area set up for him to receive the condolences of the visiting dignitaries. After another hour, the Secret Service guided Hastings to his limousine and the car took off slowly and headed for the hotel in nearby Johnson City, where he would spend the night before flying back to Washington in the morning.

As soon as the president left, the media coverage ended, and the hoards of press left to get back to Washington themselves. The first lady was already a news item of the past.

Kate was finishing up her day and getting ready to go home. Earlier in the day she had gone into Betts' office and checked his right top drawer for the supposed file key. It wasn't there and Kate presumed he had taken it with him. She was more determined than ever to find a way to view the contents of the unmarked drawer, but it would have to wait until another time.

Mentally tired, she picked up her purse and started for home. Her frame of mind improved when she thought of seeing Reed before too long. She wondered if he had been able to elude his tail without much trouble.

She let herself into the apartment and decided to fix a hearty dinner, for she was sure that Reed would be hungry after his long drive. Mixing up a meat loaf and popping it in the oven, then fixing some tapioca pudding and getting it in to chill, she then had time to change and freshen up.

She was still in the bedroom when she heard a knock at the door. She ran to open it, but instead of Reed, there stood Diane. Diane came in and noticed the dejected look.

"Were you expecting someone else, Kate, maybe Reed?"

"Yep, I'm expecting him any time now."

"Well, I won't hang around then, I just stopped in to thank you for the computer games. Joe and I have been enjoying them. I especially like the murder mystery one you have to try to solve."

"And thank you for the new slippers and cologne, Diane. Leave it to you to notice my old, beat up, worn slippers. I really was in need of some new ones."

"Okay, now I'll hightail it out of here and let you get on with getting your dinner. Something's smelling awfully good from the oven," she remarked.

"It's meat loaf, and I should start getting the rest of the dinner going."

"I'll see you later, Kate. Have a pleasant night," and out the door she went.

Kate made her way to the kitchen and started preparing the potatoes and the vegetables. Within a half hour, the doorbell buzzed, and she hurried to answer. Sure enough, there was Reed standing there with suitcase in hand, grinning.

"Reed, I'm so happy to see you."

She threw her arms around him and kissed him.

"Come on in. I've been so worried about you. Did everything go as you planned? Were there any problems in New York? Oh, Reed, I'm sorry, I'm running off at the mouth. Come put your suitcase in the bedroom, and I'll fix you a drink."

Laughing, Reed said, "Is this the way I'll be greeted every time I have to make a trip? If so, I like it."

Taking his suitcase into the bedroom, he dropped it on the floor and reached to take Kate in his arms. He kissed her long and hard, then nuzzling her neck he whispered, “Kat, my sweet Kat, all the way here I thought of holding you like this. I’ve missed you, love.”

“I’m happy that you did,” and as Kate started to go on, her nose picked up a burning smell coming from the kitchen. “Oh my gosh! The meat loaf!”

She tore out of his arms and made a dash for the oven.

“Whew, close call,” she called over her shoulder. “Hope you like your meat loaf with a crust on it,” she laughed.

“I’m so hungry I’m not going to complain about a little crust on my meat loaf. Besides, I think I rather prefer it that way.”

“Good, now sit down and tell me everything while I finish the rest of the dinner.”

She fixed Reed his drink and continued with her task while Reed told her all about his trip. He told her that all went well until he hit the interstate for home, then how Betts’ man outsmarted him by going unnoticed until he caught up with him at the diner.

When Reed told Kate about the car chase and the guy trying to force him off the road, she was riveted to the spot. He finished his tale by telling her of his knocking the other car off the road and it going end over end till it burst into flames. Kate went over to him and checked him over for bruises.

“You’re not hurt are you, Reed?”

“No, sweet Kat, I’m thankfully all in one piece, and I don’t want you to worry. The guy is dead and burned, so there will be no tales carried to Betts. Even if he does find out about his dead agent, he will have no idea where I am. So, now we’re going to forget that it ever happened and get on with our dinner. I’m famished!”

When they sat down to eat, Kate decided to hold off on her news till later. Satisfied that Reed was indeed all right, she tried to make the meal as pleasant as she could. When they were finished, Kate sent him into the den while she cleaned up the kitchen.

That done, she fixed Reed another drink and poured herself a glass of wine, then went into the den. Reed was stretched out on the couch with his eyes closed. She sat their drinks on the table and bent down to gently caress his face with her hand. He reached up and pulled her close and they shared a long, tender kiss. Kate, knowing that she had to tell Reed of the planned cabal, broke away.

“Reed, I want to tell you about the reports I’m doing for Betts—the documents that he wants done by Friday.”

Raising up to a sitting position, he saw that her face was grave.

“When I talked to the general, he said you would have something to tell me.”

Reaching down for his drink he sat back and said, "Okay, Kat, let's hear it."

She took a sip of her wine and started in. For the next two hours she talked, disclosing everything she had read about the systematic takeover of the country.

Reed sat sober-faced, listening. Every once in a while he would question something he wanted clarification on, or let out a low whistle. When Kate finally finished with her dissertation, she sat quietly studying Reed.

"It's unbelievable what this man is plotting. Some of this has been out there for those of us who took the time to understand its meaning," Reed said. "I've written columns on several of these things you mentioned, trying to warn the public to wake up and realize that they were slowly and methodically losing their freedoms. Sorry to say, not many took note. Seems John Q. Public was too busy enjoying the good life."

"I know, Reed, and now it may be too late. This plot has got to be squelched!"

"All we can do," he said, "is try our best shot. And you, my green-eyed Kat, may be in danger, walking around with this knowledge."

"Betts has sworn me to secrecy with the threat of dire consequences should this leak out. I'm frightened Reed, but I'm more frightened at the prospect of this coming about. We have got to stop this somehow."

Leaning over, she rested her head on his shoulder, snuggling up against him. He put his arm around her and held her close. They stayed that way quietly for a time, then Reed uttered,

"I'm going to see the general tomorrow. He has the Pentagon blueprints and wants to tell me something about them. I'll relay all you've told me to him. We only have three days left to figure out how this can be stopped. But right now, my love, there's nothing we can do. I think it's time we got to bed and put our minds on something much more to our liking."

Kate told Reed to go on ahead and she would join him after she took care of their glasses. When she entered the bedroom, Reed was undressing.

"How would you like to join me in the shower, Kat?"

"Sounds intriguing. I accept," she grinned coyly.

For the next half hour, the two lovers enjoyed an arousing, sensual time, each taking turns slowly caressing and washing each other's body. By the time they finally found their way to bed, their bodies were craving for more. And more they got, as they molded together in love's embrace.

Chapter 12

Kate sat at her desk typing, bracing for Betts' return. Around eleven thirty he made his appearance, looking relieved and pleased with himself. She stopped working and greeted him.

"Did everything go well, Mr. Betts?"

"Yes, yes indeed, Kate, everything went as scheduled. Of course, the president is feeling the brunt of his loss, but he'll hold a short press conference this evening to thank the country for their heartfelt sorrow over the demise of the first lady. He wants the people to know that he intends to push ahead doing the work of the country. He also intends to inform them that he's making every effort to bring Murabi to justice. We can't have that idiot terrorist roaming loose around the land."

"I'm sure the president must be hurting deeply," Kate said with all the sympathy she could muster.

"I've got some work to do and then I'm going home for the day," Betts put in. "I need some rest after a very trying trip. Tell me, Kate, how are you coming along with those documents?"

"Just fine, Mr. Betts. There'll be no problem having them ready for you by Friday noon, if that's all right."

"Yes, yes, that'll do just fine. What do you think of our master plan?

"Well, it sounds very impressive, but I don't understand how you hope to accomplish such a feat."

"Yes, yes, it is spectacular, is it not? As for carrying it out, well Kate, that's for us to do and for you to witness when it comes about," he smiled sneeringly.

"It does seem rather a tall order to just lay on the country," Kate dug on. "You don't expect the people will just except this out-of-hand, do you?"

"Enough talk of this, you'll soon see how easily it's done. Now, I must get my work done and leave," he said as he vanished into his office.

Kate took time out to go for lunch, and by the time she returned, Betts had left. Hoping against hope, she again checked for the keys, but they still were missing, so she proceeded back to her desk and continued with her distasteful job.

Spread out across the desk in General Powers' home office were the original blueprints of the Pentagon. The general was just escorting Reed into his office to view the plans.

"Reed, these blueprints are the original ones from nineteen forty-three. I've been studying the floor plan and found nothing that would gain us entry into the Missile Launch Center, or the secret meeting room. The walls are all steel enforced, and there's no way to break through. However, look at this." He pointed to an area leading off from the Pentagon itself.

"It looks like it could be a tunnel leading from the building," Reed said. "Could it be something they decided not to complete for some reason?"

"It is completed, Reed. This is an underground tunnel. If you follow my finger here, you'll see that it starts out below the Missile Launch Center and travels out in this direction. Here it shows an in-ground entrance, almost at the river's edge. After further probing, I found out that these entrances—here and here," pointing them out to Reed, "had been sealed up after the second world war ended. The tunnel was put there as an escape route, if needed. Its Pentagon entrance is in the storage room below the Launch Center. There are about a dozen steps leading up from the storage room into the Center. Now the door from the Launch Center to the storage room remains unlocked. They keep supplies down there now, so it is a regularly used stairway. However, the storage room entrance to the tunnel was sealed off at the same time as the river entrance. I myself have seen it. It's solid steel, and no one has access to it or has even questioned it."

"Go on, General," Reed urged.

"I've got several men out there as we speak. They've located the in-ground river entrance and have broken the seal. They've been careful not to be seen, but they're in an area quite safe, bordered by the Potomac. They've been able to follow the tunnel to the steel door that opens into the storage room, but that's as far as they've gone with it. At this time, I have them making sure that the tunnel is safe and passable. They're going to take acetylene torches in there tonight and tomorrow night to go around the door breaking the seal. Small junctures will have to be left on each side to hold the door in place. Reed, I don't know what the president has planned, if anything, in the Launch Center, but I want access to it if need be. I've had this uneasy feeling about those changed coordinates that I spotted when I was in there the other day. It just doesn't figure for them to be different than they have been. I'm going to position men in the tunnel Friday night just as a precautionary measure. What do you think?"

"I think it's an excellent idea and possibly a very smart move, General. I commend you on you're logical deductions, and you hit the nail on the head when you stated that we must not overlook any possibility where this president is concerned. Kat gave me the complete rundown on the takeover plan of these maniacs."

For the next hour, Reed filled him in on the highlights of the president's takeover procedures.

"Reed, this country is doomed if he gets away with this atrocity. By the way, we picked up Betts' conversation with Kate earlier. She tried to get him to reveal something about their plot, but he wouldn't bite. She's sitting in a precarious position where they're concerned. At least until midnight on the thirty-first, then she won't matter to them since everything she knows will be put into effect."

The two men talked for another half hour discussing their helplessness in case "terrorist" bombs were in the works. There was just no word on where they may be set up.

"All it's gonna take, General, are a few well-placed bombs to declare martial law—subways, New Year's Eve concerts, casinos—any number of locations that would cause the disastrous effect he's looking for. Midnight, the year two thousand, millions of people will be out celebrating."

"I know, Reed, and if we don't stop it somehow, there could be loss of life to millions of Americans," he added somberly.

Vowing to keep at it until the last minute, the two shook hands and Reed left for Kate's apartment. He had to pick up his things from the night before and get on back to his own place. Having driven by several times to check for anything amiss, he figured that Betts still thought him to be in New York City.

Kate swung open the door when she heard him knock.

"You're just in time for dinner," she smiled.

Reed gave her a big kiss and told her to lead the way. She set out the broiled steaks, baked potatoes, green salad and fresh baked rolls. Pouring them each a little wine, they sat down and enjoyed the delicious, juicy steak dinner.

Kate told him about her day, and Reed proceeded to fill Kate in on what he had learned from his visit with the general.

"What do you know," Kate ventured, "an underground tunnel leading from the Pentagon to the banks of the Potomac. I've never heard of it," she mused.

"I doubt there is anyone left in Washington that has," Reed replied. "There's no doubt in my mind that neither the president nor his goons have the faintest idea it exists, which only helps our cause."

"Does the general really think the president is stupid enough to order the deployment of a nuclear bomb to back up his plan if need be?"

"There's no second guessing what a mad man will do to gain power, and knowing as we do, that Hastings has already done-in his wife, bets are that the lives of millions of citizens aren't going to deter him one iota. And now, my green-eyed Kat, what's say we clean up this mess and catch the president's press conference?"

"Betts has already told me the gist of what is to be said, but I'd like to watch anyway."

In a jiffy they had the work done and Kate fixed them each an after dinner drink. The two made themselves comfortable on the couch and flicked on the television to see Hastings stepping up to the microphone.

He started out by thanking the people of the country for their heartfelt support during his time of sorrow.

"He uses just the right amount of inflection in his voice to make the listening public feel his professed pain," Kate said with a smile.

"He's an excellent actor, as he should be, after all the years of practice he's had pulling the wool over everyone's eyes," Reed supplied.

They listened on while the president talked about his "loving" wife and how not only he, but all Americans would miss this wonderful woman. Reaching up and wiping a tear from his eye—one Kate couldn't detect as even being there—he looked at the camera straight on and vowed that he would move forward with making the country's business his first priority. Finally his diatribe over, he took a few questions from the press.

"They're really playing soft ball with him tonight," Reed put in, "even more so than usual. This "Hastings" Press has been the biggest villain in this whole façade. They've protected him from everything that came down the pipes that most likely would have opened the eyes of the public to his subversive tactics. Now this country, very soon, may witness this president's high treason. One thing you can bet on—his faithful press will fall right into step if this comes about," he finished.

"It's finally ended," Kate said. "I don't know when I've ever heard the press "kissing up" so bad. Thank heaven for the few that do have integrity and try to get the truth out there to the masses."

Reed leaned over and gave her a meaningful kiss and said that he must be leaving. He went into the bedroom and gathered his things while she waited in the hallway with his coat in hand. They kissed good night and Reed was gone. Kate turned out the lights and went in to read herself to sleep. She would not sleep well this night.

Chapter 13

Waking up in a cold sweat, Kate jumped out of bed and ran to the phone. When Reed sleepily answered, she felt contrite for waking him.

"It's Kate, I'm sorry to wake you, Reed," she got out shakily.

"Kat, what is it, are you all right?"

Wide awake now, he told her to go on. Hearing his soothing voice calmed her down and she started in.

"Reed, last night I had a nightmare. It's the fourth time in the last two months that this same, identical nightmare has occurred."

She proceeded to tell him about the chase, the briefcase and the gunfire.

"I believe the last street I'm running down to be your street Reed, though I can't be sure of that. But, last night's dream was different from the others. At the point where I hear the last crack of gunfire, I saw myself falling and then I saw this blinding explosion! Reed, it was mammoth in size, spread over the land, and there was total devastation," she finished breathlessly.

The other end of the line was quiet.

"Reed, are you listening?"

"Yes, Kat, I am. From what we know of these "Sensitive" powers of yours, this sounds as though something of the worst kind is about to happen. Kat, I want you to calm down and try to put this out of your mind. Don't try to figure it all out right now. All we can do is try to go on to figure out what Hastings has planned and get it stopped! But, my love, I want you to be extremely cautious in the next two days, do you hear me? I don't want you taking any chances with your life, do I make myself clear?" he emphasized.

"Yes, Reed, I feel quite calm now that I've gotten this out. And I promise to watch my step. What can you make of it?" she asked.

"I don't know love, but I don't like it. You've proven to be very accurate in these dreams and visions of yours. I'm meeting the general today out at the river entrance to that tunnel. I'll tell him what you've relayed to me and get his thoughts on it. I'm going out there to see where exactly this entrance is located and take a look through the tunnel itself. I'm telling you this, Kat, in case you need to get hold of me, you can reach me on my cell phone."

"All right, Reed, but I'm sure I'll be okay. I've got a full day of working on those hideous documents. I told Betts that I'll have them finished by tomorrow noon. Now, I'd better go and get ready for work. You take care too, won't you, Reed?"

"Yes, sweet, I'll phone you after my show tonight."

"I'd like that. Good-bye, Reed."

Kate plugged away at her task, hoping with every word she typed that these insidious documents would never see the light of day. She took a longer lunch hour than usual, tired from three constant hours of continued typing, thinking she deserved the time away.

Slowly making her way back to her office, she couldn't help but feel the quietness around her. All offices had been shut down as of yesterday till after the New Year holiday. Wryly, she thought, "If this madness isn't stopped, they may never open again, at least not for the same purpose as they are used now."

About mid-afternoon, Betts came sauntering in to see how she was progressing. She assured him that it was moving along and would certainly be ready tomorrow by noon, if not a little sooner.

"Fine, fine," he murmured.

"These folders of documents are finished, sir, if you would like them now."

"No, no, I'll wait until they're all completed. I prefer to keep them together and not take a chance on misplacing one somewhere."

"Very well. Have you and Mrs. Betts made plans to celebrate the year two thousand?" she quizzed.

"No, no, nothing special. I have a late meeting tomorrow, and then we'll see what follows. I'm sure you've made plans to ring in this very special year, haven't you?"

"Why, er, of course," Kate quickly lied. "I have an invitation to a special celebration. It sounds like it'll be a grand affair," she continued. "But for now, I'd better get back to the work at hand if I'm to finish on time."

"Yes, yes, of course," and with that he left the office.

"Quick thinking, Kate old girl," mentally patting herself on the back.

Down at the banks of the Potomac, under much security, Reed and the general were discussing Kate's dream.

"I've related it to you just as Kat told it to me, General. What do you make of it?"

"This is worrisome, Reed, I certainly have to give it credence. Kate has proved herself in this area and I don't think we should take it lightly. Have you warned her to use caution?"

"Oh, yes. I stressed that point with her."

"As for the mammoth explosion you just described, it could be a nuclear blast. I don't know, I just don't know, Reed. One thing for sure, we need to definitely man this passageway and be ready if anything does occur. More than ever, I'm getting a queasy feeling. Well, there's nothing we can do at present, so let me show you what we have here. We have easy access to the tunnel from this point of entrance. See how it's naturally camouflaged from view? It's completely out of sight from anyone who would happen to be in the area."

The general had one of his men lift up the door and they descended the steps into the tunnel. Reed noted that it was a good eight feet wide, and about seven feet high. The general's men had placed battery-run lanterns along the length for easy going. The electricity to the tunnel had of course been turned off since its sealing. Coming to the exit door into the storage bunker, the general motioned to Reed to keep voices to a whisper.

He pointed out the work that had been done the previous night with the torches. Noting that they had gotten about half way done with breaking the seal, he thought that they should have no trouble getting the rest finished that night, except for the areas that would hold the door in place. Reed nodded his head in acknowledgment, and the two retreated through the passage.

"This is a godsend," Reed remarked, as he climbed out onto level ground. "You've done a tremendous job setting this up, General. Whatever happens, this should be kept secret, don't you agree?"

"By all means, Reed, this may be very important to us in the future."

"Thank you for taking the time to show it to me, but now, I should be going. I just about have time to have a quick bite to eat, then get over to the Studio to set up my program for tonight."

"I'm on my way home, so I'll walk with you to our cars," the general said as he fell in step beside Reed.

Kate had finished her day without incident, and was now home, having a quick microwave dinner. She had to get some bills ready to mail out before she settled down to watch Reed's program. She remembered it dealt with Y2K and was interested to hear what the experts would have to say. She busied herself with her chores, and soon was curled up on the couch waiting for the show to begin.

The program got under way, talking about the different objectives that had been put into place to prevent any major problems.

Reed questioned the panel about the fact that many of the large cities had set up bunkers of one sort or another to accommodate the leaders in case of Y2K problems, or in case of terrorist threats, nuclear threats, or any other disasters.

He pointed out that New York City had one in a high-rise, and was set up with bulletproof windows and everything else needed in those times of crisis. He also mentioned that an emergency bunker had been set up in Ohio at a military base, and Los Angeles had one five stories under the city hall.

Reed asked the members of his panel if indeed there was no big worry with Y2K, as per the White House, then why were all these cities taking such drastic precautions. Was it because they really expect something other than Y2K glitches?

They each took turns answering, then went into other areas, such as the problem that Russia thinks it may have with it's nuclear system come two thousand. On they talked as Kate listened intently.

At the home of Jason Betts, a private telephone conversation was in progress.

"Will? Jason here. I took care of that little surprise you asked for. Yes, yes, our nosy Mr. Adams will be getting his warm welcome home greeting very shortly. We'll be killing two birds with one stone, as the saying goes. We send Adams a message and we send by way of television the message that our "mad" bomber is still out there terrorizing the country. Okay, Will, stay tuned to your set. Good-bye."

Brad hurriedly lifted the receiver and dialed the television station. Getting a connection, he fairly shouted the warning. "Get everyone out of the studio, there's a bomb to go off! Do it now! This is General Powers speaking. Hurry!"

He slammed down the phone and yelled to Helene, who was in watching Reed's show in progress.

"Get Kate on the phone, now!"

Helene jumped up and dialed Kate's number.

"Why, Brad, what's going on?"

Kate lifted the receiver and just as she was about to say hello, the loud boom came through the television set. The stage that the panel sat on fell into pieces, and rubble was flying everywhere, then nothing. The station went dead.

Helene and Kate both stood watching in disbelief while still holding the receivers to their ears.

"Reed! Reed!" Kate screamed. "Oh my God, no!"

Helene was yelling through the phone at Kate, trying to calm her, although she herself was in shock.

Brad grabbed the phone from Helene and forcefully started talking to Kate. When Kate heard the deep voice it made her realize that she still had the phone to her ear. Brad could hear her sobbing and he kept talking loud to her trying to get through.

"Kate, this is Brad! Listen to me. Are you listening, Kate? Speak to me Kate, now," he ordered.

Still crying, she whimpered into the phone. "Reed, a bomb, my God," her weak voice sobbed out the words.

"Kate, you listen to me. I'm on my way down there. I'll see what's happened and if there are any casualties. You sit tight, do you hear? I'm sending Helene over to your place right now. She'll stay there with you, and when I find out anything about Reed, I'll call you immediately. Did you get all that Kate?"

"Yes," she sobbed, "I'll wait here for Helene. Please hurry now, General, and get word to me right away."

"I'm on my way and so is Helene. G'bye Kate."

He hung up the phone and both he and Helene grabbed their coats and keys and were out of the house like a shot.

Chaos was taking place at the television station. When the general pulled up and parked a half block away, he took off on a run. Viewing the scene, he saw bodies being loaded into ambulances and fire trucks trying to douse the flames. It was utterly devastating.

His heart sank as he witnessed more casualties being taken from the building. Some were coming through the rubble on their own, holding different parts of their bodies that had been injured by flying debris.

His hopes rose when he spotted one of the guests Reed had mentioned was going to appear on his show. He raced over to the man.

"Mr. Feldmann, can you tell me, is Reed Adams injured? Do you know anything about his circumstances?"

The dazed man was trying to get his bearings and tried to focus on the words. It was obvious he was in shock. Feldmann finally spoke.

"I'm not sure. We were in the back of the building, so didn't take the full blast. The lights went out, rubble flew everywhere," he trailed off.

Just then a paramedic came up to him and looked over his head wound.

"We'd better get you to the hospital and get that tended to. Come with me and we'll get you in our truck."

The general moved on and finally found a fireman helping people out of the rubble.

"Sir, do you know anything about Reed Adams? Have you seen him?"

"Just saw them taking him and some others to the hospital," the man shouted. He was walking under his own steam, but he was pretty badly cut up, looked like to me."

"Thanks."

The general took off for his car and hurried to the nearest hospital, parked his car and ran in the entrance. Hurrying to the first desk he saw, he inquired "Was a Mr. Reed Adams brought in with the bomb casualties?"

The nurse checked down the list and lifted her head.

"Yes, he's here. They have him in Emergency."

"Which way is it," the general asked, and she pointed out the direction to him.

"Thanks," he threw over his shoulder, as he tore down the corridor, bursting through the door.

He started making the rounds, checking each bed for a familiar face. Not finding Reed, he was about to ask a nurse passing by, when he spotted him sitting in a chair with a young Doctor tending his wounds.

"Reed, thank God," he exclaimed.

"Hi, General."

"How bad did you get it?" the general asked.

"From what the young doc here says, I have a good-sized cut on the back of my head, and these cuts on my arms. Oh yeah, and a pretty good gash on my lower leg," holding it up a bit.

The general could see his pant leg was pretty well torn to shreds, both from the blast and from the doctor taking the scissors to it.

"When he gets finished stitching you up, I'm taking you to Kate's. She's beside herself. I sent Helene over to stay with her. I'm going to call right now and let her know you're okay. I'll be back in a few minutes to get you," and out the door he flew.

He found a desk phone and asked permission to use it. Getting a nod, he dialed nine and then Kate's number. She answered immediately.

"He's all right, Kate, just a couple of bad gashes and some cuts and bruises. He's at the hospital and they're cleaning and stitching him up now. As soon as they're finished with him I'm bringing him over to your place, but we'll have to stop at his apartment first and get him into some clean clothes."

"Thank heaven! Thank you, General, I'm feeling a whole lot better now. Helene has calmed me down. We'll have the drinks ready when you get here. Please hurry," she finished.

"Will do, Kate. Fill Helene in and we'll see you shortly."

About fifteen minutes later the two men were on their way.

Back at Kate's, she and Helene were sipping their drinks and watching the news. Diane had dashed over earlier and saw that Kate was in her mother's care. She didn't stay long because of a pressing engagement.

The news was full of the bombing. They were showing pictures of the demolished building and getting interviews with anyone they could grab hold of to tell their story. They were reporting twelve people killed and nineteen injured. It was the work of a terrorist bomb, no doubt, the reporter stated. They latched on right away tying it to the dreaded Jabar Murabi. Kate and Helene exchanged glances.

"You and I both know who's responsible for this, Kate. I'm not going to say anything though. We'll wait to hear from Brad. He knew that bomb was to go off seconds before it did."

"I know, Helene, it's more than obvious. But you're right, no sense speculating when we'll find out the truth of it soon enough."

Another ten minutes went by, and finally the ladies heard the sound of men's voices in the entrance way. Making a mad dash, Kate jerked open the door and threw her arms around Reed.

"Ouch, careful Kat, my love. You've got a bruised up guy on your hands."

"Oh, Reed, I'm sorry! Have I hurt you?"

She led him gingerly into the den with the general following, to where Helene was waiting. Helping him down into a comfortable chair, she handed over his drink. After Kate checked over all his wounds and was satisfied that they would heal in a short period of time, she began to relax.

They were ready to hear the story; the real story of what took place. The general told them of the overheard conversation between Betts and the president.

"I tried to warn the station in time, but it was too late and now twelve more innocent people have met their deaths at the hands of this fiend in the White House."

"Let's hope they believe that their message came across loud and clear," Reed said. "I can't have them dogging my every move."

"Well, you two, Helene and I have to be on our way. Try to get a good night's rest. Something tells me we're going to need it."

Good nights were said, and they were on their way.

Kate and Reed talked a while longer, then Kate shooed him off to bed and followed behind. They both took a few minutes in silent thoughts for the victims of the night's disaster and gave thanks for the lives that were spared. They fell off to sleep with their arms wrapped around each other.

Chapter 14

In the president's quarters, Hastings sat in conversation with his visitor.

"Well, this is the day we've all been working toward, Manning. I've spent twenty years of my life preparing for this. You don't know what it's been like, having to play the people, the Congress, the world. I'm sick to death of promoting myself as the people's missionary. I've had to pour billions of dollars into giveaway programs and humanitarian causes. That's the secret to getting elected here in this country, Manning. Keep them all on welfare. Dole out free food, unemployment, and medical, and they beg for more. They love their benevolent government. They're so brain dead, they can't even see that they've already lost their rights as a free people. All of those on welfare, won't even see any change come tomorrow. It's all the others, the capitalists, the workers, that will feel their demise. Hah! They've all been so busy stuffing their pockets with the booming economy, they don't care what their president does. Seeing them fall is going to give me the most pleasure."

"You certainly had them all figured out from the git-go, Will. Tell me, what are you going to do with Quinlan? He's back in town. Do you expect any trouble from him?"

"Choosing Quinlan for my running mate was a stroke of genius. The guy is so far out in left field that he couldn't find his way back to the dugout if they gave him a compass. I'll just dissolve the vice presidency along with Congress, and he'll retreat back to Massachusetts. A year from now he'll still be wondering what happened. As for today, there's a big White House celebration for the New Year. It'll be televised, and I've asked him to do the honors. It was only fitting, since I just lost my devoted wife. No one expects me to attend. He and June will be fully occupied."

Sitting back puffing on a cigar, he put his feet up and watched the smoke swirling in the air.

"General, this plan is perfect, and you're to be commended for bringing it to my attention. No aftermath destruction to clean up, and it will no doubt go unnoticed by the masses till it's too late. Yes, Genesis is the perfect solution."

"Everyone has their orders and are standing ready," Manning put in. "I don't foresee any complications."

"All right then, let's sit tight, and then meet with the others at eleven. We'll all want to be there to witness our Rebirth!"

Reed, quickly hanging up the phone, re-dialed.

"General, Reed here. I just got a call from someone on the inside who wouldn't give his name. He said he heard of plans in motion to set off bombs in five different locations tonight. I don't know how valid this is, but we can't afford to ignore it. He said they're to go off simultaneously. Here are the locations he gave me. The one to cause the most worry is the Times Square Building. There'll be thousands of people out there to ring in the New Year and to see the ball drop. The other four are Chicago's O'Hare Airport, Caesar's Palace in Las Vegas, Los Angeles International Airport and Disney World in Florida."

"Maybe this is the break we need, Reed. I'll dispatch teams to those areas right away."

"Good. I'll catch up with you later, General."

While at the office of the National Security Council, Betts was keeping busy in his office, waiting for Kate to finish up her work. He was on the phone to his wife when Kate entered with the stack of folders.

"I've got to go now, Caroline, I'll see you when I get home."

He hung up the phone and took possession of the New Order files. When he reached up to take them, Kate saw that he wasn't wearing his bugged watch.

"I notice that you're wearing a different watch, Mr. Betts. Did something happen to the one I had fixed for you?"

"Yes, yes, they did a sloppy job of putting the crystal in, and it fell out last night, so I had to leave it home for Caroline to take it in and have the crystal put back in right. I suppose I can get along without it for a few days."

He glanced over the files and then told Kate "Your job is finished here, so go and enjoy your New Year, and with it, the new beginning."

"I hope you enjoy your New Year holiday also, Mr. Betts. I'll see you on Monday then?" she questioned.

"Without a doubt, without a doubt."

She turned, went back to her desk, collected her things and left.

"Weird little habit he has of saying everything twice," she mused as she made her way out the door.

Glad to have the time, she stopped by the market to pick up her extra food supply. She found the store quite depleted of supplies, but she gathered up whatever she could.

"Seems many others are preparing for Y2K also," she thought.

She was able to get four bottles of water, some nutrient bars and several different kinds of canned goods. Arriving home, she lugged her heavy bags in and neatly stacked everything in the pantry.

"I'd better give the general a quick call and let him know about Betts' watch," she mused, and dialed up his number.

Helene answered and spoke with Kate for a few minutes before getting the general on the line.

"Hello, Kate," he said, "how are you doing? You're not having any problems, are you?"

"No, General, I'm okay, it's just that I thought you should know that Betts isn't wearing the watch. He said that the crystal fell out, and it would take a couple of days before he got it back."

"Well, there goes our chance to listen in on their meeting tonight, and we were hoping to get some much needed information. It can't be helped. Thanks, Kate, for letting me know. I'll call the men off the bug, and I'll close up shop here."

"All right, General, good luck tonight."

"Thanks, Kate, good-bye for now."

After getting herself a bite to eat, she placed a call to her grandparents.

"Just wanted to call and wish you both a happy New Year, Gram," she said, trying to keep her voice cheery.

"Well, dear, we wish the same to you. Gramps isn't here right now, so I'll relay your wishes to him when he comes home. Kate, we saw that awful explosion last night. Is Reed all right?"

"Yes, Gram, he's fine. Just a few gashes and cuts. He was very lucky, there were so many lives lost."

"They're saying that it was a terrorist bomb," Maggie added. "I don't understand why they can't apprehend those vile people. From what I read in the newspaper, the whole country is jittery wondering where they'll strike next. Enough about that now Dear, when are you coming to visit again?"

"Probably not for awhile, but I want to tell both you and Gramps thanks for the wonderful Christmas. You two outdid yourselves to make Reed comfortable. Both of us had a most enjoyable time. I've got to go now Gram. Will you tell Gramps I'm sorry I missed him?"

"Yes dear, I will. You take care of yourself."

"I love you both and I'll talk to you soon."

She hung up the phone and plopped down on the couch. Thinking maybe a jog would be the thing to get her mind active, she went in and changed into her sweats and running shoes. Grabbing her keys and transistor she headed out.

As she started off down the street, she took little note of the car pulling away from the curb. Continuing along her usual route, while crossing a street, she waited for a car to pass.

"That's the same car I saw pulling out from my street," she mused.

Catching sight of the same car out of the corner of her eye from time to time, Kate had to acknowledge that she was being followed.

"Betts sure as heck is behind this," she thought. "He's not leaving anything to chance. Well, let the jerk follow me; if I'm going to have a miserable New Year's Eve, then so is he," and with a little burst of speed she continued on her way.

Sure enough when she arrived back at her apartment, the car pulled in to an open parking spot about three doors away. Going in and locking the door behind her, Kate went to the phone and dialed.

"Hello."

"Hi, Reed, this is Kate. Betts has put a tail on me. There's nothing to worry about, I just want to let you know in case you had any idea of stopping by. If they were to spot you coming in here, they might panic, and that could be trouble for both of us."

"Good girl, Kat. You just sit tight and bore the guy to death. I'm glad you called. We got some information on possible bombings tonight. Said he was an "inside" informant. We don't know how reliable it is, but the general has sent teams out to check out the target sights."

"Do you think it's valid information Reed? I question it because they know you were trying to pry out information about terrorist threats. That's why they put the tail on you the other day. It sounds fishy to me that someone would contact you about it. You don't think it could be just another ploy to keep you out of their hair a while longer, do you?"

"It very well could be, Kat, but we dare not ignore it. If it is on the up and up, many lives could be saved."

"I don't know if you've spoken to the general in the last couple of hours, so I'll tell you myself," Kate said. "Betts wasn't wearing the bugged watch today. Seems the crystal fell out, and he had on another one."

"The general did relay that to me. That's a stroke of bad luck for us, but we'll keep plugging. Well, Kat, I've got a late business dinner, then I'm coming home to change and wait around till it's time to join the general at the tunnel around eleven o'clock."

"I'll let you go, Reed. Please be careful. I love you."

"I love you, my little sharp-eyed Kat."

Kate got up to finish preparing her dinner and turned the volume up on the television so she could hear in the kitchen. She listened as they described the different planned galas and celebrations. There was one that was to take place in D.C. They said that Quinlan, the vice president, would fill in for the president, who was still in mourning for his wife.

"The perpetrator mourning for his victim," she thought. "How he has manipulated everyone, even me for a time."

Shaking herself back to the task at hand, she fixed a plate of pasta and sat down to eat.

Later, after clean-up, she made her way to the shower, then put on some fresh clothes. A niggling of a plan was beginning to form. She couldn't get the locked file drawer out of her mind.

Sitting on the edge of the bed, putting on her comfortable tennis shoes, and idea came to her. She jumped up and walked around the room thinking as she paced. She remembered that she had left her empty briefcase at the office earlier.

"That's the excuse I need, if anyone were to question me," she surmised. "I've got to see what's in that file drawer."

She ran to the closet for a jacket and then to the kitchen. Reaching into a bottom drawer she pulled out a screwdriver. She found a piece of stiff wire and stuck both in the pocket of her jacket. She had already decided that her tail wouldn't interfere. He was just there to follow her. She grabbed her purse and keys and shot out the door.

Noting that she was indeed being followed, she drove on toward the White House at a safe rate of speed. Parking her car up close, she got out and headed for the door.

"Kate? What are you doing here at this hour," Jim asked.

Pulling out her pass, she explained to the guard that she had forgotten her briefcase and had come to collect it.

"There's some paperwork I have to do over the weekend, and Mr. Betts wouldn't be happy with me if I didn't finish it," she remarked with a grin.

"Well, go ahead on in," he told her, and Kate hurried through the door.

"So far, so good. Now to work fast so he doesn't wonder what's taking me so long."

She ran into her office, picked up her briefcase and hurried into Betts' office. She quickly checked the top right drawer of his desk, not really expecting to find the keys, but there they were! She almost yelped for joy. Grabbing them, she dashed to the file cabinet.

"Oh, please be the key that fits," she mumbled.

Click! Excitedly, she pulled open the drawer and sifted through folders. Her eyes landed on what she was looking for. Genesis! Quickly removing the file, she opened it and scanned through.

"This is it! The whole plot is right here."

Frantically, she stuffed the file into her briefcase.

"I've got to get this to Reed."

She shut the drawer, and replaced the keys, and headed out the door. Just as she started down the corridor, Betts loomed in front of her.

"What are you doing here, Kate? I thought you had a party to attend."

"I have, Mr. Betts. I put my invitation in my briefcase, then went off without it earlier. I really must hurry home to dress."

"Well, move along then."

Kate hurried toward the door, pushed it open and rushed by Jim.

"I've got it Jim, thanks."

Just then alarms started going off all around her. Jim rushed to the door, and Kate took off on a run for her car. Her hands shaking, she fumbled in her coat pocket for her keys.

"Calm down, Kate, get hold of yourself," she muttered aloud.

Just as her key turned and the engine roared to life, she spotted Betts yelling for her to stop. The car jumped as she jerked out of the parking lot and into the street. She saw the headlights of a car turning out of the parking area behind her.

"Oh God, my tail, I forgot about him. Keep your head about you, girl. Think of the fastest way to Reed's apartment."

She kept talking aloud to herself, hoping it would keep her calm. As she tore down one street, then another, terrified, she saw that her pursuer was gaining.

"Not too much further; hold on Kate!"

Just about three blocks from her destination, she heard the sound of rapid gunfire, then a loud POW! One of the bullets had blown her tire. The car skidded and swerved erratically, almost flipping due to the high speed. Kate gripped the wheel and stomped her foot down on the brake. She screeched around a corner and got the car stopped in the middle of the road.

Grabbing the briefcase, out the door she flew, taking off at a dead run. Behind her she could hear a car skid to a halt, but it didn't stop soon enough, and rammed into her car which sat blocking the road.

Kate turned her head and saw the man climbing out, gun in hand, after her. Putting forth all the effort she could, she ran wildly down the street. Just as she tore around the corner onto the street where Reed lived, she heard another crack just as she stumbled and went down.

Arriving home from his business dinner, Reed stepped out of his car and started for the front door to his apartment when he heard gunfire. He stopped short and ran back to his car. Getting in he started the engine and reached into his glove compartment for his gun.

He sped down the street and saw a woman running with a man not far behind her. He saw her stumble and fall, just as he turned and came sharply to a stop. He jumped out of his car, now setting sideways in the middle of the road, took aim and fired.

He saw the man fall to the ground and ran up to him. Blood was spurting from the man's neck, so he knew that he was dead.

Reed ran back to the woman, knowing in his gut that it was Kate. She lay sprawled out on the pavement. He checked for blood, but could find none, except for a cut on her forehead. He turned her over gently.

"Kat, Kat!"

He was just about to pick her up when she stirred. Her face was ashen and blood was trickling down from her forehead. She opened her eyes.

"Reed, thank God. Get the briefcase, where's the briefcase," she uttered as she tried to sit up.

Reed glanced around and spotted it by the curb.

"It's here, Kat. You'll be all right in a minute. You've bumped your head. Take it easy, love," he soothed.

"Reed, there's no time; the papers, they're in the briefcase. Genesis. We've got to stop them."

"Can you sit on your own?" he asked.

She pushed herself up and tried to pull herself together.

"Stay here. I'll get the briefcase, then get you in the car."

After placing both Kate and the briefcase in the front seat, he ran back and pulled the dead man into some bushes at the side of the road. Coming back to his car, he jumped in and started off.

"Betts saw me, Reed. He knows I have Genesis.

"You can't go home, Kat, they'll be waiting for you. And my apartment isn't the safest place at the moment. We'll get you over to the Powers' and get you fixed up."

They pulled up to the general's residence in record time and hurried as fast as Kate could go. She was nearly herself again, but had a banging headache. The general opened the door, took one look at Kate and herded them in. Helene immediately took in the situation and rushed

Kate to the bath to clean her wound. She handed Kate a warm cloth to wash her face, then put some salve on her cut and a large bandage across the gash. She got Kate a couple of aspirin, and they joined the men in the den. Reed sat Kate down on the sofa and handed her a brandy that the general had poured.

"How're you doin', love? Feeling strong enough to tell us what's going on?"

Kate nodded. "Get my briefcase over here and open it up. Inside you'll find the Genesis folder. Please hurry Reed, there isn't much time before they carry out their plan."

Opening the case, Reed reached in, pulled out the folder, and began to read.

"My God, we've had it all wrong," he all but shouted. "This isn't an inside terrorist plot as we suspected. General, come here and look at this!"

"Good Lord," the general remarked.

The two men sat reading through the folder, then looked at one another.

"Kat, you've done it! You've given us the information we need to get this stopped," Reed said.

The general left the room to make a couple of phone calls and Reed explained to the women what was in the file.

"I won't be able to get into the finer details, but here it is. They're planning to fire a nuclear war head missile straight up over the country, detonating five hundred kilometers above the Iowa, Nebraska state line at exactly midnight. This detonation will produce high energy gamma radiation that, interacting with the air molecules, will produce charge separation that ejects recoil electrons and leaves behind more massive positive ions. The earth's magnetic field interacts with the recoil electrons which further radiates electromagnetic pulses or EMP as it's called. A burst on the order of five hundred kilometers in altitude, over the spot they have chosen, will cover the entire continental United States."

Reed rushed on. "Electromagnetic pulses will induce multiple simultaneous electric and electronic system failures. That means power grids, telecommunication networks, transportation systems, water supply systems and a host of other things will be shut down. I won't go into anymore, except to tell you that something like this could last a year or even several years. Sweet, isn't it—no loss of life, no destruction to clean up—just the total shut down of the country. The first thing Hastings will do is declare martial law, and move on from there, pronouncing himself supreme ruler of the land."

The two women sat silently trying to take in the workings of EMP when the general returned to the room.

"I've called off the bomb teams, and notified the others at the tunnel that we'll be there shortly. Reed, we've got one hour to get over to the tunnel, finish unsealing the door and put a stop to this madness. The others will meet us there. We already have our men in the tunnel. Helene, I want you to leave the house till this is over. Check into the Phoenix Park Hotel for the night. I'll come there and get you."

"Kat, you should do the same. I don't want you anywhere near your apartment tonight," Reed ordered.

"I won't be, Reed, because I'm going with you and the general. You don't think I've come this far just to bow out before the grand finale. Don't say anything, Reed, I'm going, and that's final!"

"All right, Kat, but you'll have to stay in the tunnel. You're not going into a possible confrontation."

Everything settled, they sped on their way.

The "big five" were congregated in their meeting room.

"Is everything set as planned?" the president asked the group.

They all nodded except Betts. "We've got a small hitch," he said nervously. "It seems that my very faithful secretary has made off with my Genesis folder. I went in to pick it up tonight and she was on her way out of the building. She said something about leaving her briefcase when I questioned her. I proceeded in to get the file, found it missing, and set off the alarm. She got away, but the Secret Service man I had tailing her sped after her. I'd bet by now that he's caught up with her and taken care of the situation. Even if she got away, there's nothing she can do with the information."

"Geez, Betts, what were you doing leaving that laying around?" the president said in disgust.

"I had it locked up tight, Will. She couldn't have known it was there. My guess is that she was snooping around and found it by accident."

"Well, we aren't going to worry about her," remarked the president. "I don't think she's smart enough to outwit a Secret Service man. We'll station a few extra men out in the hall just to play it safe. Did you set up Adams like I told you to?"

"I did," answered Betts, "and the report is that he fell for it. The poor sap would have jumped on anything having to do with terrorist bombs."

"All right then. Preston, I assume the troops are ready to take command around the country?"

Preston nodded in the affirmative.

Hastings continued on. "I want them in the streets as soon as the effects hit the ground. The good citizens that are up and partying will be too drunk to care and the others will just think it's Y2K glitches and go to bed. What a surprise they'll have in the morning. Well, shall we all head down to the Missile Launch Center?" he grinned.

Opening the door, the "big five" procession moved along toward their destination.

Down at the Potomac River entrance, the general and Reed were in conversation with the men.

"I want everyone filled in on what's transpiring here," the general commanded. "Is the magnet in place on the door?"

"Yes, sir, it's in place and ready to pull out when the last seal is broken. The men are down there now finishing it off. It should be ready to go when you give the order."

"Excellent work!" He looked at his watch and saw that they had seven minutes to get the job done.

"C'mon, Reed, let's get underway."

"You got it, General."

The men had their weapons ready and headed down the tunnel. Kate was running along side of Reed and had her orders to stay downstairs in the storage room.

Five minutes to go when they reached the door. Giving the order to pull it out, the men charged through into the storage area and up the stairs. They burst through the door and ordered Gobels away from the controls. The president and the four others moved to one side of the room.

"What's going on here?" the president raged. "I command you to stop this at once!"

The outer door to the hall burst open, and the firing of guns erupted.

"Kill them, kill them all," the president roared.

Gobels leapt to the control board with three minutes to go. The general jumped him and a fight ensued. Gobels lunged for the button and set off the missile, then a shot fired, and he fell dead.

The general reached for the coordinates and quickly changed them to what he hoped would render the nuclear missile harmless. The general's men finally overpowered the president's, and there were many lying dead on the floor.

They looked around and restrained the president and the others. Hastings had taken a bullet in the shoulder and was holding on to the wound, while Preston lay dead beside him. Hargraves and Manning threw down their guns and had their hands in the air. Betts was nowhere to be seen.

Down below in the storage room, Kate hid herself behind a supply shelf.

"Please, oh please, let them be in time," she prayed.

A few minutes later she heard someone running down the steps, and peeked out.

"Betts!" she silently shouted.

Before she had time to think, she jumped out in front of him. Startled, he swung and caught nothing but air. She kicked at him trying to knock him down. Catching her by the hair, he pulled her to the ground.

"You bitch, you bitch," he spat at her. "I'll kill you," and he grabbed her throat in his hands and squeezed.

Kate struggled and kicked. Remembering the screwdriver, she worked it out of her pocket and plunged it into Betts' side. Yelling, he fell off her onto the floor writhing in pain.

Kate sat there trying to get breath back into her lungs, when Reed came running down the stairs. Taking in the scene, he pulled Betts up and smashed his fist into the man's jaw. Betts fell to the floor out cold.

"Kat, baby, are you all right? Did he hurt you?"

"I'm okay, just need to get my breath. What's happening up there?"

"They're all rounded up and in custody of the general. They got the bomb away, but the general changed the coordinates. We're waiting to see where it ends up. And you know about Betts here. Seems that my green-eyed Kat also has nine lives," he smiled.

Kate, feeling her strength returning, got up and the two of them made their way up the steps. Reed sent someone down to get Betts and the general made a phone call.

"Get the vice president on the line immediately," he ordered.

"Yes, this is the vice president."

The general explained as quickly as he could what had just taken place and asked Quinlan to meet him in the Oval Office at the White House. The general moved over to the control board and saw that the bomb had exploded over the Pacific Ocean.

"I'm afraid I didn't get it out far enough," he told Reed and Kate. "It looks as though it's going to affect parts of the coastline, but it won't be anything drastic. A few power outages, and so forth. Hopefully, it won't last long. Right now, we get these traitors locked up, and get over to the White House. The vice president's waiting!"

Chapter 15

Reed and Kate were on their way home. There was nothing more for them to do now that the president's coup had been thwarted. It looked as though very little damage would occur along the coast from the launched missile. The general and his men would get with the vice president, and the country would be told the truth of what happened.

Reed took a glance at his watch.

"Well, Kat, it's twelve-fifteen, year two thousand. We're still a free country." He grinned over at her just as she bolted upright in her seat. "What is it, Kat? Bringing the car to a stop, he reached over and took hold of her. Kate had turned pale and fear filled her eyes.

"Heaven help us," she exclaimed. "Reed, the nuclear blast that I saw, it wasn't Hastings! It's something else, something much worse! This blast that I saw was over land, not in the upper atmosphere! The giant explosion, the mushroom cloud, the devastation!"

"Good God," Reed uttered. "Kat, are you sure?"

With tears streaming down her cheeks, she nodded her head up and down.

"Yes, I'm sure!"

Reed turned the car around and made a dash for the Oval Office. They found the vice president and General Powers listening to a report coming in on the speaker phone. They moved closer to hear the cataclysmic news.

The vice president was being informed that China had declared war on the United States! They had launched nuclear missiles, and had hit their targets of San Francisco and New York City. Both cities were consumed by the holocaust, and millions of lives lost.

Immediately, Quinlan made several calls. Ordering retaliation with everything available, he told his chiefs of staff to squash China, and to get it done quickly. He ordered all American troops home from foreign shores, except those that were based where they could retaliate with air power against China.

While he was talking to General Langwell, the Secretary of State and others made their way into the Oval Office to render advice and assistance to the ill-equipped vice president.

General Powers and the others sat down to discuss strategy. They informed the vice president that the first order of business was to knock out China's missile launch sites. Issuing the orders as the others advised, Reed and Kate hoped that Quinlan would hold up under the tremendous pressure.

They could see that there was nothing for them to do, and so told General Powers that they were leaving.

"Good luck to you all," Reed said, and Kate acknowledged the same hopes, and then they departed for home.

Arriving at Kate's apartment, they found total destruction.

"Betts' men were here looking for you and the briefcase," Reed said. "You can't deal with this tonight, Kat. C'mon, we'll go to my place. I've got some phone calls to make, and you can tune in to the latest reports that come in. There'll be no sleep for us tonight."

The two weary, downhearted warriors made their way across town to Reed's apartment. They picked up Kate's car at the side of the road where someone had pushed it to get it out of the street. Reed changed the flat tire, and other than being pretty banged up, it still ran well.

Pulling the cars up to park in front of the apartment building, the two hurried up to let themselves in the door.

Reed got them a much needed drink, then went to make his calls. Kate turned on the television and sat down to hear what was being reported.

"I've phoned Helene and told her not to expect the general any time soon, and filled her in," Reed said when he made his appearance.

"They're reporting that we have wiped out the Chinese shipping compound in Los Angeles, California. They suspected that the missile that targeted New York City was launched from there. Also a few minutes after midnight, China took command of the Panama Canal, and they have shut it down to all ships. General Langwell has our Air Force en route to wipe out the Chinese positions there, so that they can get the Canal opened to afford passage to our ships."

Reed and Kate sat glued to the television, wishing that they could do something to help.

While back at the White House, all the leading heads were trying to coordinate their efforts to retaliate and make strategic decisions.

"We're dropping everything we have available on them, hitting not only the missile launches and silos, but targeting every official headquarters and military base," General Powers stated to the others. "We've got to knock them flat, and quickly. Hopefully the Chinese premier, Hu Chao, will be eliminated in one of those blasts," he added.

It was early morning. Because most of the country was just waking up, and had no idea of what was taking place around the world or of President Hastings' diabolical plot, the vice president was preparing for a special television address to the people of America. The cameras and microphones were almost in place. In a few minutes, Quinlan had to face the country with the devastating news.

"Citizens of the United States. I want you to know what has taken place. Shortly after midnight, January first, the year two thousand. The President of the United States, Willard Hastings, has been thwarted in his midnight attempt to overthrow the government of this country. His plot to declare martial law and assume dictatorship was quashed. He and others involved have been put under arrest. I, as your vice president, will now attempt to lead the country through the horror that has befallen us. China has declared war on the United States of America. They have launched nuclear missiles which have hit New York City and San Francisco. Manhattan is in ruins, as is a good part of San Francisco, including the Golden Gate Bridge. Millions of Americans have lost their lives and millions more will be affected by radiation fallout.

"The United States has deployed counterattack missiles and it is reported that they are blasting China off the face of the earth. We are retaliating with everything we have, hoping to bring this mass destruction to a swift end. Martial law will be declared, but only in those areas of destruction. The National Guard and FEMA will take command of rescue and maintaining order. Do not attempt to enter these zones. Those people caught looting will be dealt with harshly. I warn all citizens to stay away from radiation infested cities. All possible help has been dispatched. I urge all citizens to donate food, clothing, blankets and medical supplies to their Red Cross centers to help care for the victims. And I urge you all to pray."

Reed and Kate had gotten a few hours sleep, and had gone over to Kate's apartment to see what they could do to clean it up. Both worked for a couple of hours getting back some semblance of order. Kate fixed them something to eat and they discussed their plans.

"Kat, I'm going to have to pack and leave for New York City. I don't know if I'll be able to even get near enough to find out anything, but I have to try. I've got to get back to work and cover this. It's my job as a commentator and reporter. Are you going to be all right here by yourself?"

"I'm going to have my car checked out. If it's in good running condition, I've decided to pack up some things and leave for Elmira. I need to be with Gram and Gramps, and maybe help with the volunteer work in the area. They're going to need all the help they can get collecting supplies for the bombing victims. There's nothing I can do here. I'll call Helene before I go and tell her of my plans."

"Well, my love, we'll have to put ourselves on hold for a time, but I want you to stay strong. We did our best to save our country from anarchy, and we did that much. We couldn't know that outside forces were waiting for the opportune moment to take their shot at us, although there were indicating signs that should have alerted us to it. It's done and now we have to put our efforts into helping the victims of this atrocity. We'll make it through this, and as soon as I can, I'll contact you. I want you to be careful on the road, Kat. You're going to run into a lot of congestion up around that area with the exodus from the city."

"I will, Reed. I'll take the round about route to avoid all I can."

"All right then, I've got to get going."

He took Kate in his arms, gazed into her somber green eyes and quietly said, "I love you, Kat. I'll be with you just as soon as I possibly can."

"Take care darling," Kate murmured. "Come back to me soon. I love you, Reed."

They shared a long, loving kiss and then he was gone.

Midmorning, and reports were coming in to the White House. Immediately, word was passed on to the press, and there was continuing coverage on every television station. Americans were in shock. News commentators reported what they could on events taking place around the bombed area. The country was put on alert to prepare, in the event that more Chinese missiles should hit. All were stunned, asking how this could have happened.

A short time after three o'clock in the afternoon, came the report that the Air Force had demolished the Chinese strongholds at each end of the Panama Canal, and that our forces had now taken their position there. The Canal was open once again, to give our ships free access.

Kate listened as she drove north to New York State. Another report blared out that San Diego had been hit with a nuclear missile. The target was the naval shipyards, but much of the city had been engulfed by the holocaust. Kate prayed for an end to this nightmare.

As she drove and listened, she wondered how she could have missed the signs. There was certainly enough proof that crossed her desk pointing to the Chinese gaining strongholds in and around the United States. The stolen nuclear secrets that were quickly covered up by the

Hastings administration, the hacking of the Pentagon computers; it all added up.

"But I was too busy trying to find out what Hastings and his cronies had planned," she chided herself. "Why had Hu Chao chosen that particular time to do his dirty work? It's as if he knew this country would be caught off guard, that we would be vulnerable," she mused aloud. "Of course! All those good will trips of Hastings to China. He must have been boasting to Hu Chao about his New Year's coup, probably promising him more access to America, more trade and who knows what else."

The sun descending, Kate pulled gratefully into the driveway of her grandparents' home. She grabbed her suitcase and ran through the back door yelling her arrival. Maggie was cleaning up in the kitchen and grabbed a towel to dry her hands while Pat came on the run from the den.

They took turns hugging Kate, then both started talking at once, asking questions. Kate couldn't help but laugh. She sat them down and explained everything to the satisfaction of both.

"But now, I must make a phone call. Gramps, could you get the rest of my things out of the car please?"

Pat nodded and hurried to his task.

"Will you excuse me, Gram?"

"Surely Kate, we'll talk later. You go get your business done."

"Hello?"

"Helene, this is Kate. I've just reached home and I felt the need to call you about something. I've had plenty of time to think on my drive up here, and I believe I've stumbled on to a possible theory as to the timing of China's mission to destroy us. I think that Hastings may have taken Hu Chao into his confidence, you know, on all those trips he made over there. My belief is that Premier Hu Chao was making his own plans to subvert Hastings' plot by using that to give this country a surprise of his own. He must have figured that nobody here would be paying attention, what with the martial law that Hastings would be busy with, and the rest of the takeover. I don't think he expected that Hastings' plot would be foiled, and I'm sure that he is stunned by the retaliation that we were so quick to deliver. It all fits right along with the Chinese long-term vow to destroy the United States.

"Helene, they never planned anything other than to overthrow our nation. They've just been going along patiently through the years, biding their time, and the time was last night. They had to have known about Hastings and used him as their patsy. Helene, can you get word to the general? Possibly he could get Hastings to admit it, if he pretends to already know what happened between the two men. I know this knowledge won't help end this war, but it would validate the reason for triggering it off at this particular time," she finished.

"Kate, I'll talk to Brad as soon as we hang up. I believe you may have found the exact cause of this war. Everyone in the country was so preoccupied that the signs were overlooked or just ignored. Did you hear about San Diego getting hit?"

"Yes, I heard, Helene. Pray that this ends soon before millions more are lost. I'll say good-bye now. You have my grandparents' phone number to reach me if you get any news to relay."

"I do, Kate. Good-bye for now."

The rest of the evening was spent in relating the president's coup and everything that happened to subvert it. Pat and Maggie were aghast at the part their Kate had played in the whole intrigue. After all of the story was told in detail, Kate, tired and beaten, retired to her bedroom and fell fast asleep.

Reed had made his way up as close as he could to the annihilation site that used to be Manhattan. All the surrounding hospitals were filled beyond capacity, and every facility that had room housed bodies of the victims. FEMA and National Guard troops were everywhere. The Red Cross had moved in to help do what they could, and people everywhere looked as though they were walking around in total shock.

He offered his help, and soon found himself in a radiation-repellent suit, helping to remove victims out of the rubble and into ambulances that were constantly on the move to and from the hospitals or makeshift morgues. There was no time to think as he continued working through the night and into the next day, until he almost dropped from exhaustion.

He removed his suit when he was out of the danger zone and gave it over to another who would take his place. They had just been working on the fringes and Reed could not help but wonder what it was like at ground zero. He slowly made his way to his car, got in and fell fast asleep.

At the White House, Vice President Thomas Quinlan was showing signs of faltering. The siege was more than a day old. General Powers was assisting him, as were many others, having to more or less take over the responsibility of making decisions. Quinlan was overwhelmed and certainly underqualified to handle such strategic commands. Never having served time in the armed forces himself, he was completely ignorant of military procedures, and clearly out of his element. General Powers conferred with the Secretary of State, and it was decided that it was necessary to keep as many advisors as possible on-hand to help the vice president with decisions.

There ended up a group of twelve men finally discussing avenues to take and advising Quinlan. Reports were flowing in to them from all sectors and things were beginning to take shape. Slowly, some semblance of order took over and plans got underway in an orderly fashion.

China was being pummeled with missiles, and they were severely feeling the wrath of the United States.

It was the third day of January when the report came in that Hawaii and Anchorage had been hit with nuclear missiles. The devastation was spreading, but the United States was on the road to annihilating the enemy.

U. S. allies, what few were left, after alienating themselves from us because of Hastings' aggressive tactics, moved in to help our cause.

On the fourth day, the Chinese were rendered ineffective. The allies and United States forces had dropped nuclear bombs on China, wiping out all of their nuclear facilities and silos.

They were brought to submission, causing Premier Hu Chao to cede. He placed a call to the vice president with his surrender. All bombing ceased and the clean-up continued. Hu Chao would stand trial for carrying out crimes of mass destruction.

U. S. allies responded by sending aid and troops into the areas of ruin. The aftermath of war had descended upon the country.

President Hastings, under the interrogation of General Powers, admitted his covert pact with Hu Chao. Having been played the fool, he was more than willing to tell all.

The good life and the booming economy forgotten, the citizens were walking around in a stupor, not able to figure out just how all of these atrocities could have befallen them.

The media seemed to have an abrupt change of alliance, and were now filling the people full of the dastardly deeds of their once beloved President Hastings. Their cover-up of Hastings did not go unnoticed by the citizens of the country however, and there was a deluge of criticism aimed at the press and media. Many well-known top commentators were fired and new, nonpartisan reporters were installed.

About midnight on January fifth, a knock was heard at the country home of Maggie and Pat Malloy. Her grandparents had retired for the night, but Kate was still up, tuned in to late-breaking news. Hearing the knock at the front door, she cautiously peaked out. Spotting a bedraggled Reed standing there, she opened the door and threw her arms around him.

"Reed, oh Reed," was all she could say.

She burst into tears of joy and Reed led her back into the warmth of the house.

"I couldn't wait another minute to see you," he rasped.

They stood in the middle of the floor embracing, not wanting to let go. Kate lifted her head up and kissed his lips.

"I'm so thankful you're all right, Reed. I've been beside myself wondering where you might be."

"The war is over, Kat, and after we get a good night's sleep, you and I are going home. We belong in D.C. Who else is going to keep a watch out for subversion! We're going to get married immediately, no ifs, ands, or buts."

"Yes, darling, whatever you say. Oh, Reed, I love you so."

"I love you, my sweet, green-eyed Kat."

Epilogue

November fourteenth, the year two thousand. The newly-elected president is addressing the nation.

"Citizens of the United States of America. I, John Stuart Jeffers, stand before you as your servant for the next four years. You have given me your trust by electing me your new president. I shall do my utmost to rebuild our country to its leadership role in the world. We have a long, hard road to travel, but we will persevere in restoring our land to its past glory.

"We must all work together, and we must undo the damage that has taken place under the greedy endeavors of Willard Hastings. I, and my vice president, Sheldon Packard, pledge you our honesty and our honor. May God help us all through these trying times.

"I want to say to one and all—and I pray you take this to heart—never allow your freedoms to be taken away because you were too busy with your good life to notice. Our freedoms, yours and mine, must not be taken for granted. My friends, on the first day of January, in the year two thousand, those freedoms were almost lost to us. Be aware, be alert and be certain that it never happens again. Thank you, and may God bless America!"

Accepting the thunderous applause, the newly-elected president slowly strolled from the podium, turned, and gave his vice president a wry grin, and a veiled, knowing look.